MURDER IN SPA CITY

A SAM LAWSON MYSTERY
BOOK 7

DAVID K WILSON

Cover design by Caroline Johnson
Author photo by Greg Johnson

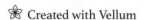 Created with Vellum

1

HER SCREAM SHATTERED the early morning silence and echoed throughout the large house.

Just minutes earlier, Charlotte Cannon had awoken with a smile for the first time in months. She had stretched her body awake, then rolled over to face the empty side of the bed. She had thought nothing of it. Her husband, Frank, always woke up earlier than her and was probably already in their home office on his second cup of coffee.

She lazily slid up and turned, sitting on the side of the bed where she was greeted by her sleepy reflection in the mirror that sat above her vanity. The late August morning sun had just peaked above the distant Green Mountains and was already shining through the large eastern-facing windows, its golden hues spreading over the large bedroom. Charlotte smiled in the mirror, happy with what she saw. Thanks to a healthy lifestyle, expensive anti-aging creams and a bit of plastic surgery, no one would ever guess she was 68 years old. She combed her long, platinum grey hair with her fingers and took in a deep breath. Ready to start the day, she grabbed a silk robe that lay at the foot of the bed and slipped it on, tying the sash loosely around her slender waist.

She looked around her luxurious bedroom and was overcome with gratitude for all her family's good fortune as she lazily began to plan her day. First up would be breakfast. It wasn't often they were all under the same roof in the morning and she wanted to celebrate. She would have Estelle, their live-in help, concoct a banquet of eggs, bacon, pancakes and cinnamon rolls.

Charlotte opened her bedroom door and began to casually walk down the long hallway, taking in each of the oil portrait paintings and assorted vacation photos that adorned the walls. She tip-toed past a couple of doors where her children were sleeping and smiled when she saw Frank's office door was open. Predictable as the sunrise.

She turned into the office with a purr and a smile, then froze in place.

"Frank?"

Her husband was sitting at his desk, but his head

was face down on it. A dark crimson liquid was dripping off the desktop, forming a large pool of blood on the Persian rug.

A panic swallowed Charlotte, leaving her numb as she dropped to her knees and began to scream.

2

ONE DAY EARLIER...

"Come on! Come on!" Sam Lawson yelled over the chain-link fence.

The horses galloped past the finish line and Sam ripped up his ticket with a groan. He looked over at a couple celebrating ten feet away from him.

"Don't rub it in," he grumbled to himself.

But he quickly shook off the loss. It was only a $2 bet anyway. He turned toward the throngs of people all enjoying the hot August day. He was surprised how packed the racetrack was for a Wednesday. For the most part, it was a casual mix of people. Lots of shorts, jeans and T-shirts. But there were still plenty of "Biff and Buffys" dressed in their pastel linens, light blue blazers, or floral dresses. And, of course, fancy hats. If you were a people watcher, there was no shortage of characters to keep you entertained.

Sam turned back to the track. He had only been to the horse races a few times, but when you were in Saratoga Springs in the summer, he had been told it was the thing to do. And Sam could completely see why. As soon as he had walked through the entry turnstile, he was surprised by the number of people camped around park benches with coolers and small tents. Closed-circuit TVs were positioned around the park area, broadcasting the races. There were people of every age and from all walks of life – families, large groups of friends, some dressed up and many dressed down. It looked more like a block party than a sporting event and was definitely not what he had expected at a racetrack. And this was all before he even entered the main grandstand.

Once inside, Sam had found a spot right along the chain link fence that separated the spectators from the dirt track. It put him right in the middle of the action, and when the horses thundered past, he could feel the ground shake.

He pulled a racing program from his back pocket to see which horse would rob him in the next race. He had no idea how to read the program and, honestly, didn't care. He picked his choices like he did most things in life, by following hunches. And he never bet more than five bucks a horse. His method showed consistent results. He was four races in for the day and had lost every single one of them.

Walking back into the grandstand area to place a bet, he took a detour to the men's room, where an old-school bathroom attendant was handing out paper towels to everyone after they washed their hands. Sam accepted the paper towel from the elderly man with an awkward thank you, and the man beamed back at Sam.

"Good luck out there, sir," he said with a wink.

"Good luck in here," Sam replied.

He emerged from the men's room to find a long line had already formed at the betting counter. Sam picked his "lucky line," which just meant a different one than the last race, and studied the racing form for a winning name.

"Got a good feeling about any one of them?" a voice asked from behind him.

Sam turned around to make sure the question was directed at him. A man standing in line behind him was smirking back at him. His tousled light brown hair and casual demeanor didn't match his clothes. Khakis, a pink dress shirt and a light blue tie. He looked like he was going to an Easter service. At least he wasn't wearing a jacket. Sam never understood men who voluntarily wore jackets in the summer.

"Sorry," the man said. "Just seeing if I can piggyback on your picks."

"Believe me," Sam replied. "My picks would get you nowhere."

The man laughed.

"Is that a bit of a Texas twang I'm picking up there?" he asked.

Sam smiled and nodded.

"You caught me," Sam replied. "Up here for my sister-in-law's wedding."

"Let me guess. You're hiding away at the track while your wife does wedding chores."

Sam laughed.

"I may not be that good with the horses," Sam said. "But I'm not completely stupid."

"I'm Donny Stanton," the man said, extending his hand.

"Sam Lawson."

"Welcome to Saratoga, Sam."

The men made small talk as they moved up in line. Never one to pass up a pun, Sam put $5 down on a horse named Mine Flies. He tried not to look surprised when Donny dropped $100 on the same horse.

Sam didn't have time to make his way back down to the fence, so he opted to watch the race on one of the large screens near the betting booths. Donny watched with him and both yelled in victory when Mine Flies finished first. Sam immediately got back in line to collect his winnings and noticed Donny just put his winning ticket in his pocket.

Clearly, he doesn't need his winnings to keep betting, he thought.

"Listen, me and my business associates are up in the 1863 Club," Donny said. "You should come join us. Great seats. AC. Private bar. And you can cash in up there without the long lines."

"If all that is up there, then what the hell are you doing down here?"

"So I can hear the chatter. You'd be surprised at the long shots I've caught from a little eavesdropping."

Donny turned and headed toward the exit.

"Come on," he said. "We have to get in through a different entrance."

3

SAM GOT a little concerned when Donny led him out of the track through one of the exits, but Donny assured him they just needed to go in a different way. Sure enough, the two men had walked no more than twenty feet when Sam spotted the attendant standing in front of a glass door. Sam could already tell he was in VIP land.

Donny showed the man his ticket and introduced Sam as a close family friend while shaking his hand. Sam had the feeling that money was being exchanged in that handshake. The attendant smiled and opened the door.

They climbed the stairs that opened into a large bar/restaurant. Dressed in a dark brown, western-cut button-down shirt and jeans, Sam immediately felt very underdressed. There were no shorts and T-shirts up here. Practically every person was well-dressed. Many of the men were wearing suits. And all of the women wore dresses, most wearing some pretty bizarre hats. The average age was decidedly older, too.

Toto, we're not in Kansas anymore, he thought.

Donny directed him over to the table of three men comparing notes in their racing forms. They looked up as Donny approached.

"There you are," the youngest of the three men said. "How did your spy mission go?"

The men laughed and Donny laughed with them. "Guys, I want you all to meet Sam Lawson. He's visiting from Texas."

"Donny, what did we tell you about picking up strays?" the larger of the old men teased as he stood and extended his hand to Sam. "I'm Frank Cannon."

Frank gripped Sam's hand firmly and shook it like he was closing a sale. He was a big man, barrel-chested and easily 6'5". His booming voice and wide smile only added to his larger-than-life presence. Normally, Sam would have been wary of such a person, but for some reason, he instantly liked this guy.

The younger man stood.

"I'm William Cannon."

William was a tall man in his early forties who looked like a younger, smaller version of Frank. William pointed to the older man wearing a very expensive suit. "This is Arthur Gilford."

Gilford nodded and leaned across the table to shake hands.

"I hope Donny didn't bring you here against your will," Frank joked.

Sam assured him that he didn't. There was something about Frank that looked familiar.

"How do I know you?" Sam asked.

4

FRANK LAUGHED.

"I guess you don't have to be up here long before you see my face somewhere," he said.

William grabbed a glossy racing program from the table and flipped it over, revealing a full-page ad for Cannon Autos that featured a picture of Frank smiling ear to ear.

Sam pointed at it in recognition. "That's what it is," he said. "I saw you on a billboard or something."

"And probably a commercial, too," William added. "He's kind of hard to miss."

"Personality sells, Son," Frank said as they all sat back down. "Paid for your college education."

"That and 110 dealerships all over upstate New York and the Midwest," William countered.

Sam put it all together. "Frank Cannon. Cannon Autos. So, it's your dealership."

"It's ours," Frank replied. "I'm the face and CEO, but William here is COO and Donny is our money guy. Arthur is our chief counsel and legal advisor and one of my oldest friends."

"Please don't hold that against me," Gilford said with a smirk.

"What about you?" Frank asked. "What part of Texas are you from?"

"East Texas," Sam answered. "Quinton. Town about the size of Saratoga."

"I bet that's pretty country," Frank said. "What do you do in East Texas, Sam?"

"I'm a cop...," Sam caught himself. It was an old habit that was hard to break. "I mean, I used to be a cop. I'm a private detective."

"Really? What kind of cases do you handle, Mr. Lawson?" Gilford asked. "Corporate espionage? Background checks?"

"Spying on people to find out if they're cheating?" Frank added with a grin.

Sam laughed and shook his head.

"I guess, at this point, pretty much anything that's thrown my way," he said. "I haven't been doing it too long. So far, it's mainly been murder cases."

Donny snapped his fingers and pointed at him.

"I knew it. I knew you looked familiar," he said. "Sam Lawson. You caught that big serial killer, right? The Replacement Killer. I just watched that true crime documentary on Netflix."

Sam nodded. After the arrest of Ed Mullen, a serial killer who had murdered dozens of Texas women over decades, a film crew had set to work on creating a docuseries on the case. Sam and Carla had agreed to interviews but thought nothing of it until it debuted on a streaming channel and soon became the surprise hit of the summer.

"I remember reading something about that," William said.

Sam smiled and tried to appear modest as he nodded. But truth be told, this was his first recognition outside of Texas and he was enjoying his new mini-celebrity status.

"What are you all talking about? Is this true crime stuff?" Frank asked. "You know I'm a sucker for that."

Donny enthusiastically offered a rundown of the documentary, looking it up on his phone.

"It's called Death Has No Substitute. It's about this guy known as the Replacement Killer who was one of the most notorious serial killers in history, but nobody knew about it for years. And, get this, he used to be a cop. And not just that, he was Sam's old partner."

Donny went on to explain how Mullen had tried to

frame Sam for the murders and then even faked his own death and eventually abducted Sam's girlfriend.

"This guy here tracked him down, though," Donny concluded. "Found him in the middle of nowhere, even when the FBI couldn't."

"Caught the killer. Saved the girl," Frank added, turning to Sam. "Is it all true?"

Sam nodded. "It was pretty accurate. I mean, they made Carla look a little more helpless than she really was."

"Carla?" William asked. "I'm guessing that's the girlfriend."

Sam lifted his hand to show his ring. "Ex-girlfriend. We made it legal right after that whole ordeal."

Frank whistled. "I need more details. But first, we need another round of drinks."

5

THE NEXT MORNING, Sam opened his eyes slowly and immediately felt confused. He had expected to see the window overlooking his backyard back in Texas, but instead was staring into darkness. As his eyes adjusted, there was just enough light to make out an oil painting of a horse on the wall.

As the clouds of sleep began to clear, Sam remembered he wasn't at home but in a hotel. He rolled over, expecting his arm to land on the warm body of his wife. But his arm fell flat on the sheet. Where was she?

"Carla?" he groaned out loud. The first words of the day dragged over his dry throat and came out in a half cough.

He propped himself up on his elbows to survey the room. The green, room-darkening curtains blocked any hint of daylight, so Sam fumbled for his phone on the nightstand to check the time. It was 7:05 a.m.

"Carla? You here?"

On cue, the hotel room door clicked and light from the hallway bathed the room as Carla walked in with two cups of coffee.

"Hey, Babe," she said with a smile. "I see you're up."

She sat the coffees on the nightstand, kicked off her shoes and crawled under the covers next to him. As she nuzzled into his neck, Sam kissed her forehead.

"Hello, Gorgeous," he said.

"Good morning," she purred back.

But Sam could feel her leaning away from him. He didn't push it, though. He understood why she needed her space. Having been abducted and tortured by a serial killer, had taken a physical and psychological toll on Carla. More than she was willing to admit. She still ran hot and cold to his touch, sometimes pulling away completely and other times feeling extra affectionate. They had been seeing a counselor to help them deal with her PTSD, and he had learned she was more affectionate when she felt in control of the situation. Like she had been the night before.

Carla pulled herself up so that she was leaning back on the headboard. Once situated, she grabbed one of the coffees. Sam followed her lead, pulling himself up, and Carla handed him the other coffee.

"You do know the way to my heart," Sam said. "And after last night, I feel like you know your way to a few other places on my body."

"Last night was very, very nice," she said with a smile.

"It was definitely in the top five," Sam said.

"Oh. You're rating them now?"

"Only the ones worth rating," Sam replied with a mischievous grin.

"So, some of them haven't been worth it?"

"Shouldn't we always strive to do our best?" Sam teased. "I do feel like we may need to practice more."

"I know, Sam," she said, growing serious. "I'm really sorry. I am trying."

"No!" Sam replied. "I wasn't complaining. Not a bit. Not a single bit. Everything is great. I'm not pressuring you at all. I'm just saying that, whenever you feel like it, I'm willing to have you to take advantage of me. I'm here for you that way."

Carla shook her head and laughed. The two of them enjoyed their coffee together in a cozy silence. Carla finally broke the spell.

"So, we didn't do much talking last night," she said.

"Yeah, that was kind of rude," Sam teased. "I really wanted to spend some time sharing our feelings."

She punched him in the arm playfully.

"Well, now you've got my undivided attention. How was your day, dear?"

"Thank you for asking, sweetheart," the slim brunette replied sarcastically. "Honestly, it was an entire day of crisis control. I guess the hotel double-booked the banquet room, so Vanessa and I spent the afternoon frantically looking for a last-minute replacement for her reception."

Vanessa was Carla's older sister who had recently moved to Saratoga Springs from Martha's Vineyard. She'd met a man on the island and a whirlwind romance blossomed. Now, just six months later, she had not only packed up and moved to Saratoga but was also planning a rushed wedding. Carla, of course, was more than a little skeptical about the whole affair but had given up on trying to talk her sister out of it and was now shifting to full support mode.

"Any luck?"

Carla shook her head.

"Not yet. But today we get to continue our search. Jealous?"

"What about her guy?" Sam asked.

"His name is Ray. Ray McCallum. Please learn it before the wedding," Carla laughed. "I guess he's a big real estate guy and pretty well-connected, so we're hoping he can dig something up."

"Just do me one favor," Sam said.

"I know," Carla replied. "Make sure the hors d'oeuvres include pigs in a blanket."

"Just something edible," Sam said. "Pigs in a blanket, Swedish meatballs. Buffalo wings."

"All the classy foods."

"All the *classic* foods," Sam corrected. "Trust me. It's what people really want."

Carla shook her head.

"What about you?" She asked. "Tell me about your day. From your texts, it sounded a lot better than mine."

Sam jumped at the chance to move on from the wedding talk, and he spoke excitedly about meeting Donny and the Cannon crew at the track. He got up and grabbed a hotel magazine, flipping through the pages until he found a Cannon Auto ad. He showed it to Carla.

"This was the guy. Frank Cannon. He is exactly what he looks like. Larger than life. But nice as hell."

Sam went on to tell Carla about their conversations. When he mentioned how they recognized him from the documentary, Carla's face soured.

"Ugh. That's going to haunt me forever, isn't it?"

"Oh, I told them about how it painted you all wrong. You'll be glad to know they all now think you're a Rambo-style badass."

"I am a Rambo-style badass, and don't you forget it," she said.

"After the last race, we walked over to this amazing bar. Got some food, listened to a fairly decent band. And, get this, they picked up the tab for everything."

"Why is that surprising?" Carla asked.

"It's very surprising," Sam said. "In my experience, rich people are usually the cheapest ones,"

Sam kissed Carla on the forehead and climbed out of bed. His walk to the bathroom was interrupted by the ring of his phone. He picked up the phone and checked the number on the screen. He didn't recognize it, but he knew the 518 area code was local so he decided to answer.

"Sam Lawson here."

Carla immediately knew something was wrong by the shocked look on Sam's face. He didn't say much — just listened and nodded.

"Send me the address. I'll be there as soon as I can."

He hung up and looked at Carla.

"That was the lawyer guy from yesterday. Frank Cannon is dead."

6

THE UBER DROPPED Sam off at an enormous brick house that spanned the entire block. He marveled at the rust-red brickwork, massive chimney and white columns that held up ivy-covered archways to form a cover over several pathways. His first thought was that it looked like one of those New England colleges he'd seen in movies. Definitely not someone's house.

Sam looked around the neighborhood. There were other gigantic homes everywhere.

Toto, we're not in Kansas anymore, he thought.

He hadn't been paying attention on his Uber ride up, but he knew it was a short drive. In fact, Sam was sure he could have easily walked here. He also knew he was still on Broadway, the main thoroughfare that ran through downtown Saratoga Springs. But now, instead of retail shops and restaurants, he was surrounded by mansions. Surprised by the quick transition, Sam made a note to pay more attention when he returned to the hotel.

The house was so huge, it took him awhile to even find the front door. When he finally did, it opened before he could even knock.

Gilford emerged, pale as a ghost.

"Mr. Lawson, thank you so much for coming. I wasn't sure who else to call."

He let Sam in, and the calmness of the outside world was completely shattered by the chaos inside the house. A couple of police officers were walking down the large cherrywood stairway with their gear. Some others were standing on a balcony that looked down over the entry hall. From all the activity, Sam could tell they were finishing up and heading out.

Gilford led Sam past the living room where he saw William, Donny and what he assumed were other members of the family. They were all too preoccupied to notice him. Some of them were crying, others whispering loudly. Sam felt like an intruder, and no one made any attempt to make him feel otherwise.

Gilford ushered him past the family into a large library. Hundreds of leather-bound books lined dozens of shelves from floor to ceiling, but Sam had the feeling they were more for show than actual reading material.

"I'm still confused," Sam said as Gilford shut the door. "You said it was suicide?"

"THEY said it was suicide," Gilford replied. "But I don't believe it. Not for a second."

"No offense, Mr. Gilford, but you'd be surprised what people hide from others. Depression is a bitch."

"His throat was slit," Gilford said. "I can barely even say it out loud."

"I'll admit, that's not a very common suicide method."

"It's not Frank's style. Even if I believed he was suicidal, and I don't, he's much too efficient-minded to do that. It would take minutes, am I right?"

Sam shrugged. "If you say so."

"Frank would have used a gun. It's quick. And there's less room for error."

"You'd be surprised about that, too," Sam said. "I once knew a guy who tried to shoot himself in the temple, but he flinched. Blew his nose clean off."

He could tell that Gilford didn't find his anecdote amusing. He coughed, stood up straight and acted as professionally as he could.

"But the police ruled it a suicide," Sam said.

"They came with preconceived notions," Gilford explained. "Nothing was stolen and no one else was hurt. So, they want to wrap this up quick and wipe their hands of it."

"Why did they have preconceived notions?" Sam asked.

Gilford looked at the door to make sure no one had entered. He spoke more quietly.

"Because that's what the family told them," he said.

"Mr. Gilford," Sam said. "Are you sure you're just not in denial? Why would they say that?"

"I don't know," Gilford said. "I think they just saw his body slumped over and the knife in his hand. I admit, it's what it seems at first glance."

"But you don't buy it."

Gilford shook his head. "And I'm not in denial," he said. "I'm trying to look at this as objectively as I can. Suicide just doesn't make sense."

"Did he have any trouble with anyone?" Sam asked. "Any enemies?"

"He owns and operates one of the largest chain of auto dealerships in the country. You don't build that without making your fair share of enemies."

"Anyone stand out in particular? Someone who is capable of something like this? Because using a knife, especially like that, is pretty personal."

"Does this mean you'll take the case?"

Sam sighed.

"Can I see the body?" he asked.

7

FRANK'S HOME office was more gruesome than Sam had imagined. Blood covered the desk and dripped down into a larger pool onto the Persian rug in front of it. Frank's body was still slumped over the desk, his head turned so he was facing his left side.

"I need to check on the family," Gilford said. "Are you alright here?"

Sam nodded as he surveyed the room. There were still a couple of uniformed police officers taking pictures and one man in a frumpy brown suit standing on the same side of the desk Frank was facing.

"Are you running this show?" Sam asked.

The man nodded and scratched his double chin. Sam figured him to be in his late 40s to early 50s. He was overweight but not obese by any means. His thinning brown hair was combed over in a valiant attempt to hide his baldness but only succeeded in making him look older.

"Homicide Detective Mike Durant," he said, never looking away from the dead body. "I'm guessing you're the special consultant the family is bringing in."

"Sam Lawson," Sam said, extending his hand. "And I'm still on the fence about that."

He awkwardly dropped his hand when he saw Durant had no intention of shaking it.

"Quite a mess here," Sam said.

"I'm gonna save you some time, Lawson," Durant said, finally looking at him. "There's nothing for you to do here. Hell, there's nothing for me to do here. They only sent me because of the family name."

"So, you're pretty sure it's suicide?" Sam asked.

"Unless you can convince me otherwise," Durant said. He pointed at the Marine Corps Knife sitting on the desk. "Mr. Cannon took this knife off of that display rack."

He pointed to the credenza behind the desk. There was an empty wooden display rack with the Marine Corps emblem engraved on it. The front of the display had two slots that held up several Challenge Coins.

"He was a Marine," Sam said.

"That's not the takeaway here," Durant continued.

"That's the weapon. He grabbed it off that display and slit his throat in a single swipe."

Sam laughed. "Say that three times real fast."

Durant gave Sam a scowl. "There's no sign of a struggle. Nothing in the house appears to have been stolen. No sign of a break in."

"But the house was filled with people, right?" Sam asked.

"Family," Durant said. "No one heard anything. No yelling. No fighting. And it's not likely that someone came in while Mr. Cannon was sitting at the desk — in the middle of the night by the way — then walked around behind him and grabbed the knife without Mr. Cannon at least standing up to fight back."

The only words that stood out to Sam were "not likely".

"Look, I'm busy," Durant said. "I think we just call this what it is and be done with it. Okay?"

Sam looked around. Standing behind the desk he could see blood splatters further out than the pool of blood on the floor. Most likely from the blood spurting when the throat was first cut.

Sam noticed something else. Other than Frank and his blood, there was nothing on his desk. No computer. No work papers.

"Did y'all already clear the desk?" Sam asked.

"It is as we found it," Durant replied. "Why?"

Sam shrugged. "Who gets up in the middle of the night to work, but with no computer or work papers?"

"Someone who wasn't really getting up to work," Durant said. "See what I mean? The more questions you ask, the more it's a suicide."

"But no suicide note?" Sam asked. "Doesn't that seem odd for a family man like Mr. Cannon?"

"Not everyone leaves a note," Durant replied.

Sam could tell Durant had no patience for his speculations, and he'd find a way to shoot them down immediately anyway. And he had to admit, it did look pretty cut and dry. Still, something didn't feel right.

"Look. This seems to be sorted out and you have enough on your plate, but I can still help," Sam said. "We both know the lawyer isn't buying the suicide verdict and he's not gonna let go of this. If anything, he's going to get other members of the family questioning everything. I used to be a cop. I've been there. But I'm your ticket out. I'll pacify them. Keep them out of your hair, so you don't have to keep dealing with them. When I come up with the same verdict in a couple of days, the shock will have worn off and Gilford will be more accepting of it."

"And you make a little money off them in the process," Durant said disapprovingly. "Look. I can't stop you, but I sure as hell am not going to give you my blessing. This family just suffered a major loss and the last thing they need is someone blowing smoke up their ass."

"Oh, I don't smoke," Sam replied, his stubborn nature kicking in. Now he wanted to take the case just to piss this guy off.

8

___

As soon as Gilford walked into the living room, William and Donny rushed over.

"What the hell is he doing here?" William asked in a loud whisper.

"You asked me to make sure your father's death was investigated properly and we all know the police aren't going to do it," Gilford replied calmly.

"We don't need to be bringing strangers into this," William seethed. "You should have checked with me first."

"Did you leave him upstairs alone?" Donny whispered as well.

"You know we can hear you," chided a female voice from the couch.

It was Rebecca Stanton. At forty, Rebecca was the

middle child of the Cannon family and the only daughter. She sat slumped on the couch, her arm wrapped around her distraught mother Charlotte. She was a shell of the woman she normally was. Proud and regal, Charlotte always carried herself with elegance and class. She had been the real backbone and heart of this family. But now, she appeared pale and weak.

Rebecca's eyes were partially hidden behind her long, blonde hair. Hours of tears had left them swollen and bloodshot.

"You had no right to do that on your own," William said, no longer whispering but still talking quietly.

"He was my friend," Gilford said. "Long before you were even born."

"This is a family matter," Donny said.

"Then why are you involved in it?" Rebecca asked.

Donny was Rebecca's ex-husband. They had met years ago when Donny was working in the finance department of Cannon Autos. His relationship with Rebecca grew, as did his role in the company. By the time she surprised him with divorce papers, he was already CFO of the company and Frank saw no need to change that just because his daughter had grown restless. It was one of the many ways he had dismissed his daughter through the years.

"Guys, don't start fighting before I get a good seat," Peter Cannon said, entering the room with a beer.

At 29, Peter was the youngest Cannon sibling. A surprise baby, as his older brother and sister loved to point out. Spoiled and arrogant, he was a frat boy that never grew up. He acted like he resented his family's money, but he certainly enjoyed all the perks it offered.

Rebecca shook her head at Peter, but he smiled and took a big swig of beer while staring her down, making it clear he didn't care what she thought.

"No one's fighting," William said. "I just want to know why I wasn't consulted."

"I took it upon myself," Gilford said. "Your father had just died, and I saw you all grieving. I saw your mother collapsed in despair. You needed to be there for all of them. This was all I could do."

William noticed how Gilford's voice trembled as he held in his real emotions.

They were all distracted by another woman who was failing in her attempt to discreetly enter the room. It was Julia Cannon, William's wife. Only slightly older than Rebecca, she looked like she could be her dark-haired sister. She walked next to her husband, sliding the phone she was holding into the pocket of her tight jeans.

"What is he even investigating?" Julia asked. "I thought it was a suicide."

"We need to be sure," Gilford said.

"What do you mean by 'need to be sure'? William snapped. "I saw him. So did the police. It was a suicide."

"We don't know what happened," Gilford remained firm.

"What does Lawson think?" Donny asked.

Before Gilford could answer, Sam stepped into the room. "Oh, good. You're already all in one place."

9

THE ROOM FELL silent as Sam entered the room. Their undivided attention stunned him for a second. Knowing it wouldn't last, he decided to lean into his power position. He cleared his throat and furrowed his brow as he paced in front of the group.

"First off, I'm truly sorry for your loss. And I'll leave you to your grief shortly. I just wanted to tell you that, while it does appear Mr. Cannon took his own life, I still have a few questions. So, I've decided to take the case."

"Have we decided we're hiring you?" Peter asked.

"We'll hire you," Gilford said. "If this is more than it appears to be, we need to know. However, we have a few ground rules. First, your complete discretion is paramount."

"I am nothing if not discreet," Sam said. "You won't even know I'm here, and no one else will either."

"And two, this has to stay under wraps," Gilford continued. "As it is, the press is going to have a field day with this. They don't need to know a private detective is looking into the possibility of murder."

"I am just here as a family friend," Sam suggested. "I'm in town for a wedding and the Cannons are old friends from the way back machine. Is that all?"

Gilford looked around at the family to see if anyone had anything else to add.

"Good," Sam said. "I have a few ground rules myself. First, I will need to speak to each and every one of you. Alone. Secondly, I'm going to need you all to stay in town. I know this is all right out of the oven and you're still processing it, but the sooner I can talk to you the better."

"I'm staying here anyway while my house is being renovated," Rebecca offered.

"Are you putting us under house arrest?" Peter asked. "Good luck with that, Mr. Not A Cop."

"Just stay close. And reachable," Sam said. "Speaking of which, I'm going to need all of your cell numbers."

"Are we being interrogated?" William asked, stepping toward Sam aggressively.

Julia put a hand on his shoulder to calm him down.

"William," she said quietly. "Please."

"Did your father normally keep a computer in his home office?" Sam asked, ignoring William's advance.

William was visibly thrown by the question.

"I don't know," he answered.

"Sometimes," Charlotte answered softly.

The sound of her voice stunned everyone. She'd been in a half trance since finding her husband's body and had barely spoken at all.

"Sometimes he'd bring it home and other times he'd leave it at the office."

"You didn't answer my question," William interrupted. "Are we being interrogated?"

"Yeah. Why do you need to question us?" Rebecca asked.

Sam looked around at everyone.

"When I got here, I noticed you have a home security system. I assume it was turned on last night?"

"Yes, I set it myself," Charlotte said.

"Who was the first to arrive this morning? The police or Mr. Gilford here?" Sam asked.

"The police," William answered.

"And was the security system still on?" Sam asked.

William thought about it then nodded.

"Yes. I remember turning it off when I let the police in. Why is that important?"

"Because, IF Frank Cannon was murdered, and

that's still a big if, then the killer would have to be someone that was already in this house."

10

NATALIE EDGARS SCRIBBLED FURIOUSLY, pushing her shoulder-length, dark blonde hair behind her ears. The police scanner spoke in police codes, but Natalie knew a 10-56 was a suicide and the address given was the home of Frank and Charlotte Cannon. She ripped the yellow page from her notepad and ran into Mitchell Galloway's office.

"Something's going on at the Cannon house," she said.

"What's a canon house?" Mitchell asked.

"THE Cannon house," Natalie clarified. "Frank Cannon? Car guy?"

She thrust the yellow note in Mitchell's face, and he pulled his glasses from his chest pocket.

Mitchell Galloway was the news editor at WSXA,

the local network affiliate for the Capital region. He'd been running the department for ten years, the only constant in the revolving door of local news. Natalie was one of his newest reporters. A year out of college and filled with passion and ambition.

Mitchell studied the note.

"When did you hear this?" he asked.

"Right now," she answered. "On the scanner. Should I go check it out?"

Mitchell stood up and yelled into the small bullpen of reporters.

"Hammond, get off your ass and do your job!"

"Mitchell, I found it. Let me check it out," Natalie said.

"You already have an assignment for the day," Mitchell said.

"Another day at the track?" she groaned. "Please. Give me something better than all the fluff."

"You're young," he said. "You'll get your chance."

Hammond, a thirty-something reporter with generically handsome newsman features, ran up to Mitchell and the two men conspired. Natalie let out a loud grunt in protest and returned to her desk, flouncing down angrily. She knew she had to work her way up, but how was she ever going to prove herself if Mitchell never gave her a chance? Even at her freelance job writing articles for a local magazine, she was relegated to social events and local color stories.

"Don't you know the Cannons?" asked the woman sitting in the cubicle next to Natalie.

"I've spoken to Charlotte Cannon," Natalie replied with a shrug. "And the daughter Rebecca."

But the question broke her out of her own ambition, and she began to think about what had actually happened. Someone had killed themselves in the Cannon house. Was it Frank Cannon? His wife? Another member of the family?

Another reporter hung up their phone.

"My source says it's Frank Cannon," he yelled across the room to Mitchell.

"Are they sure?" Mitchell yelled back.

The reporter nodded.

Mitchell turned to Hammond. "Go. Now."

Natalie stewed for a minute, but then stood up and headed for the door.

"Where do you think you're going?" Mitchell asked.

"I need to change my clothes," she said. "Don't worry. I've got two hours until I have to be at the track."

She turned and walked out, not waiting for his permission. As she shut the door behind her, she made a mental note to change outfits before returning to the studio. Right now, however, she needed to get to the Cannon house.

11

AFTER TALKING TO THE FAMILY, Sam asked Gilford to follow him to the library.

"What you say to him, you can say to all of us," William said.

"I'm going to be asking each of you questions in private," Sam said. "So, you'll just have to wait your turn."

Julia coaxed her husband away from Sam.

"Please don't make a scene," she said quietly.

William shot her a glare but, seeing the pleading look in her eyes, immediately softened. He nodded at Sam, who nodded back in appreciation.

"Again, I'm really sorry for your loss," Sam said to the room. "I'll try not to be a bother."

He then motioned for Gilford to follow him to the library.

Gilford shut the door behind him.

"First off, I'm going to need the phone numbers of everyone in that room," Sam said.

"Please don't mind William," Gilford said. "He's grieving."

Sam waved him off.

"No harm done. And no judgement made. How long has he had a drinking problem?"

Gilford was stunned by the question.

"He reeks like a distillery," Sam explained. "And yesterday, I couldn't help but notice how much he put away."

"William's not the monster he tries to make himself out to be," Gilford said with a sigh.

"I get it," Sam said. "Living in his father's shadow. Always seen as the kid, especially if you work together. I'd get a chip on my shoulder, too."

"William's not the showman like his father, but he has a good business mind. And you're right. Frank always saw William as his son, not a peer. So, William never got the respect he craved. And that he felt he deserved."

"That'd drive any man to drink. And maybe want to do something about it?"

Gilford didn't understand the question at first, but when it sank in, he shook his head vehemently.

"Oh, William would never kill his father," Gilford said. "He idolized him."

"I've been doing this for a long time now and I've learned that there's no telling what people would do," Sam replied. "Especially where money is concerned."

Gilford smiled, looking around the the expensive furniture and opulent decorations.

"You must find all of this pretty ostentatious," he said.

Sam laughed. "This is nothing," he said. "You ain't seen crazy money until you've seen East Texas oil money."

Gilford laughed back.

"Why don't we start by you telling me about your relationship with Frank?" Sam asked.

"We were friends as far back as I can remember," Gilford answered. "Grade school, right here in town. We went to college together. I went on to law school, but Frank wanted to start making money. By the time I passed the bar, he'd already opened his first car dealership and hired me before I put my cap and gown away. I've been the family lawyer ever since."

"And work stuff?" Sam asked.

"I handle his personal legal needs and oversee a corporate legal team," Gilford explained.

"Are you close with the entire family?" Sam asked.

"Not especially," Gilford answered. "Except Charlotte. I've known her as long as Frank has. But just because I'm not as close to the children doesn't mean I'm not protective of them. My wife and I never had children of our own, so the Cannons have been my extended family for years."

"Were you with your wife last night?" Sam asked.

"My wife succumbed to cancer five years ago."

"Geez, I'm sorry."

Gilford nodded in acknowledgment, then quickly changed the subject back to the matter at hand.

"I was here for the photo shoot and then headed home after. I only live a couple of blocks away, so I walked. I was home by 9. I have security cameras around my home. I'm sure there's a record of it all."

"Wait. Photo shoot. What photo shoot?"

12

THE CANNON FAMILY sat quietly in the living room. William paced back and forth, looking at the closed library door.

"What are they talking about in there?" he grumbled.

"Honey, come sit down," Julia said, patting the empty spot on the loveseat next to her.

"Can you believe the audacity of that man?" Rebecca asked. "Accusing one of us of murdering Dad?"

"He's just trying to exploit this to take our money," Peter said. "The sooner we pull the plug on this, the better."

"Gilford had no right," William seethed.

"This whole morning is a nightmare," Rebecca said,

as more tears began to flow. "I keep hoping I'll wake up and it's all a horrible dream."

Donny, crouching down against a wall and shaking his head in disbelief, seemed to notice William's pacing for the first time.

"Bro, come on. Take a breath," he said.

"Mom, Gilford will listen to you," William said, ignoring Donny. "You've got to get him to call off this guy. It's the last thing we need right now."

Charlotte had taken Rebecca into her arms but seemed a million miles away.

"Mom?" William repeated.

"We need to trust Arthur," she said quietly. "He's always had our best interests in mind."

"Maybe he did it," Peter said with a mischievous grin. "He's in there trying to shift the blame to one of us."

"Except he wasn't in the house last night," Julia said.

Peter looked at everyone in the room.

"So, which one of us is capable of murder?" he asked.

"Not now, Peter," William said.

"I mean, clearly you are," Peter said to his older brother.

"Well, there's the pot calling the kettle black," Donny replied.

"Stop it!" Rebecca snapped. "Dad is dead! Don't any of you care?"

Peter pointed at his sister.

"You'd be the dark horse candidate, but I could see it," he said.

Julia stood up.

"You're all sick," she said, storming out of the room.

Peter looked at William and pointed at Julia, raising his eyebrows and nodding his head as if to say it could be her. William felt a need to defend his wife. He clenched his fists and started toward his brother only to be stopped by his mother's voice.

"She's right," Charlotte said. "A terrible tragedy has happened. I've lost my husband. You've lost your father. We should all be coming together to help each other through this. I need you all with me right now, but I can't take all this bickering."

She stood quickly and rushed out of the room. No one said a word. Through the heavy cloud of shame, they heard their mother run up the stairs and slam her bedroom door shut.

13

IN THE LIBRARY, Gilford recounted the previous evening's events to Sam.

"I remember William grumbling about having to do the photo shoot and Frank reminding him that publicity is part of the job."

"You say photo shoot again like I know what you mean," Sam said.

Gilford measured his words like a lawyer.

"It was part of a puff piece on Frank for a local magazine," Gilford said. "The editor thought it would be a good idea to take pictures of the entire family. Part of Frank's family man image."

"And something the family didn't want to do," Sam inserted.

"Rebecca and Charlotte didn't mind. They both

understand the value of good PR in this town. William grumbles about everything, but he's a professional and went along with the plan. Peter was the challenge."

"Why's that?"

"First, he lives in Boston, so he had to drive home. Second, he seldom returns calls or texts from his family. Probably never even reads them. But Rebecca had the idea to reach out to one of Peter's local friends and have him make the call."

"Ooh. Bait and switch. I like it."

"He arrived yesterday, while we were at the track," Gilford continued. "And Frank, William and I returned to the house after dropping you off."

"So that was about seven o'clock?"

"I believe so," Gilford replied. "The family was all here, including Julia, William's wife. Thank goodness."

"Why's that?"

"William can be an angry drunk, especially if he's forced to do something he doesn't want to. Julia's about the only one who can calm him down."

"Wait. What about Donny?" Sam asked.

"Oh, he was here, too," Gilford said. "From what I understand, he passed out on the living room couch."

"Yeah, about the whole Donny thing..."

"You mean the ex-son-in-law who the father tends to favor over his daughter?" Gilford said with a smile. "It can get awkward. Luckily, both Rebecca and Donny act like adults for the most part. It could definitely be a lot worse."

"So back to the photo shoot," Sam said.

"Right. So, we all arrived at the house. The photographer was already here setting up lights in the living room. I said hello to Charlotte."

He smiled as he said her name.

"She was beside herself with happiness, having her entire family under the same roof. Anyway, I said hello to her and made sure everyone else was accounted for. I then stayed for the photo shoot, making sure the photographer stayed within the agreed-upon limitations. Group photos and Frank alone. That was it. Anyway, that lasted about an hour, then I said my goodbyes and went home. I was having coffee this morning when I got the call at roughly 7 a.m."

"Who called you?" Sam asked.

"Rebecca. It was awful and I wish I could erase it from my memory. She was gasping in a panic, and I could hear Charlotte sobbing loudly in the room. Can you imagine? Finding your own husband dead? Like that? That poor woman."

Sam gave him a second to collect himself.

"So, then what did you do?" he asked.

"I told her I'd be right there," Gilford answered. "I got dressed and rushed over. By the time I got here, the police had already arrived."

A knock at the door interrupted them. They both turned as a uniformed officer opened it.

"Mr. Lawson?" he asked. "I've been asked to bring you to the police station."

"Right now?" Sam asked.

"I was told to tell you it's important and you need to come now."

14

A FEW MEMBERS of the press had gathered outside the iron gate in front of the Cannon house, looking for any hint of a story. A few of the cameramen were shooting B-roll footage of the house, a couple of newspaper reporters were yelling questions at the police officers still standing by the front door. None of them noticed the car parked directly across the street behind them. If they had, they would have seen Natalie Edgars slumped down in her car seat, shooting videos with her iPhone.

And while the others were focused on the front door, Natalie noticed some activity at the side door. A uniformed officer walked out with a middle-aged man she didn't recognize. He was dressed casually - a brown button-down shirt and jeans. Unassuming and definitely not anyone familiar.

Her curiosity was peaked even more when she saw him get in the passenger side of the squad car. Natalie knew who all the Saratoga Springs detectives were, and this man definitely wasn't one of them. Who was he? A family doctor? A different lawyer? A suicide expert?

Something about him struck Natalie as strange. Maybe she was reaching too hard for a story and was making things out of nothing. Or maybe she could be on to something. Either way, she had nothing to lose. It wasn't her story and what she did in her free time was up to her. She decided to follow the squad car and see if it led her to anywhere interesting.

15

SAM and the officer parked in the lot behind the Saratoga Springs Police Station, unaware of the car that had followed them. The officer motioned for the Texas detective to follow him as he walked toward a large brick building that filled an entire block. Like many buildings in downtown Saratoga, it was an old structure, steeped in history going back to the turn of the century. This particular historic building housed the City Hall and Public Works offices, as well as the main police station. The officer led Sam to a side door that took them directly into the police department, which was already bustling with activity.

"Is it always like this in the morning?" Sam asked.

"Welcome to track season," the officer laughed.

He led Sam to a flight of stairs that took them to a less chaotic but still very busy second floor. As they walked toward an office on the far side of the floor, Sam could see Detective Durant arguing with a stocky man sporting short gray hair and a large mustache. But what really caught his attention was the man's thick, jet-black eyebrows. Sam already knew he was going to have to work really hard not to stare at them.

Durant and the furry-browed man stopped arguing when they saw Sam approaching.

"Sam Lawson, good to meet you," the man said in a gravelly voice. "Police Chief Tom Morelli. Come in."

"Did I already do something wrong?" Sam asked, trying hard to stay focused on the chief's eyes.

Chief Morelli laughed and motioned for Sam to have a seat as he sat down behind his desk. Cannon remained standing in the doorway.

"Nothing of the sort," he said. "Detective Durant here was filling me in on the Frank Cannon suicide and how the family has hired you to investigate. In the spirit of cooperation, I wanted to share all the information we have."

Sam had a feeling this was less about a desire to cooperate, and more about getting Sam to back off.

"I'll be up front with you," the chief said. "We've reviewed the forensics and got the preliminary cause of death results from the coroner. If Detective Durant here believes it was suicide, and the evidence backs it up, I have no reason to believe otherwise. I don't have the manpower to second-guess every case at the public's whim."

Sam started to argue the point, but Morelli stopped him.

"Look, track season is important to this town," Morelli said. "Hell, to the entire state. Can you imagine what would happen if people thought we were investigating the possibility of a crazed killer that was breaking into homes and slitting throats?"

"That'd be bad for business," Sam said.

"I know how that sounds," Morelli said. "And if I believed for a second that Mr. Cannon was actually murdered, we'd be all over it. But the evidence is pretty cut and dry. Frank Cannon died by suicide."

"But you don't mind if I do some poking around on my own, do you?" Sam asked, catching himself directing the question at the chief's eyebrows.

"I looked into you," Morelli said. "You were a good cop. Impressive record. Now you're famous for catching a big serial killer. You even made a movie about it."

"I didn't make anything," Sam corrected. "Someone out of my control made a documentary about one of my cases," Sam said. "I didn't get paid for it and I had nothing to do with it."

"But I bet it gave you a lot of exposure," Morelli said. "And that's good for business."

"It's a pain in the ass, is what it is," Sam replied.

"I'm just saying, another high-profile murder investigation would sure be good for another show, wouldn't it?" Morelli said.

"Screw you," Sam said, bolting up. He was really beginning to dislike this chief.

"The case is closed, Mr. Lawson" Morelli said, motioning for Sam to sit back down. "But I know that lawyer isn't going to let this go. And there's nothing we can do if he's hired you to keep investigating. But this can be a win-win, right? Isn't that what you told Detective Durant? You buffer us from that family and their pitbull lawyer, and we can concentrate on actual police investigations about real crimes. But if you uncover anything about Mr. Cannon's death or otherwise, you come to us first. Got it?"

"I've got no problem with any of that," Sam lied.

Morelli smiled.

"Detective Durant, share what we have with our new friend."

Durant sighed and tossed a file in Sam's lap. As Sam skimmed it, Durant gave him the Cliff Notes.

"Official cause of death was exsanguination from a severed carotid artery. Time of death was approximately 3 a.m. The weapon used was a Marine Corps knife that had previously been displayed on the credenza behind Mr. Cannon. No other signs of injury. We're running a toxicology report but don't expect to find anything more than a high blood alcohol level, given the activities of the day and night before."

"He got up. Got dressed, went to his office, grabbed the knife and checked out," Durant summarized.

"But didn't leave a suicide note," Sam said.

Durant ignored him.

"If anyone broke in, it would have activated the home security system. And, even if it were someone in the house, it's doubtful they could have forced Frank out of bed, made him get dressed, led him to his office, then made him sit down and be quiet while they slit his throat. There are too many ways for that to go wrong."

Sam started to argue, but he knew every argument he had was purely speculative. From the facts given, it did look like a suicide. Still, something told him it wasn't that simple.

Chief Morelli stood, letting Sam know their meeting was over.

"You do what you need to do, Mr. Lawson, within the law, of course."

The two men shook hands and Durant opened the door.

"Oh, one more thing," Morelli said. "From what I

understand, you tend to ruffle feathers wherever you go.
I won't put up with that in my town. Are we clear?"

"Consider your feathers safe, sir," Sam replied,
purposefully staring at the chief's eyebrows. "Although,
you may want to consider giving them a little trim."

16

A HEAVY SILENCE had fallen over the Cannon house, broken only by the occasional clinking of glasses and bottles as the housekeeper cleaned up the dining room from the night before. Upstairs, a different cleaning crew was hard at work. At the protests of Gilford, who wanted to keep the office as is to help Sam's investigation, Charlotte insisted it be cleaned immediately.

"The images I have seared in my brain are enough," she had said. "I don't need a constant reminder every time I walk to our bedroom."

The family sat around the living room, most of them lost in their phones. Gilford sat on the edge of an oversized, brown leather ottoman, leaning forward toward the couch so he could hold Charlotte's hands in his own. No words were spoken, but years of friendship and a shared love for Frank offered a slight solace for both of them. The moment of peace was interrupted by William leaning down to Gilford's ear.

"We need to gather the board as soon as possible," he whispered. "They're going to want reassurances that the business is secure. I'll be running the company as I always have. And we need to meet with our PR agency as soon as possible to figure out how to weather this."

Both Gilford and Charlotte looked at William in shock.

"William," Charlotte sighed.

"This is neither the time nor the place to discuss this," Gilford hissed.

"You know that if we don't get ahead of this, it could be a nightmare," William argued.

"It's already a nightmare," Charlotte snapped.

William looked at his grieving mother and softened.

"I'm sorry, Mom" he said, dropping his head. "I'm just feeling like I need to do something."

"Then sit with me," Charlotte replied. "Please."

William fidgeted nervously. Sitting still was not his strong suit. He smiled gently at his mother.

"Of course," he said quietly, as he sat next to her on the couch. "I'm here for you."

But while he comforted his mother, he glared over her head at Gilford, mouthing the word "*Soon.*"

17

AFTER LEAVING THE POLICE STATION, Sam decided to check in with Carla at the hotel before heading back to the Cannon house. He walked into their hotel room just as she was walking out of the bathroom, wrapped in a plush white robe.

"I didn't order room service," she said.

"I'm with hotel security," Sam said. "There have been reports of suspicious activity in this room and I may need to frisk you. Thoroughly."

She put her arms around his neck and kissed him softly, gently biting his lower lip.

"Mmmmm," she purred. "Let's just stay in our room all day."

"Don't tempt me," he growled as he squeezed her butt.

He kissed her again and absentmindedly caressed a scar on her arm.

Carla pulled away, putting a hand over the scar and immediately trying to cover up her reaction.

"I'd love nothing more than to climb back into bed with you," she said. "But... sisterly duty calls."

Sam let out a sigh. "I've got some work to do, too."

Carla kissed Sam on the cheek. "What's going on with the dead guy?"

Sam filled Carla in on everything. How the police were calling it a suicide, but the family lawyer didn't agree.

"What do you think?" Carla asked.

"I don't know," Sam said.

He explained the murder in graphic detail and Carla never flinched. As a medical examiner, she had heard it all, and seen even more. In fact, her ME habits took over and she was soon asking Sam technical questions, like the length of the incision and range of blood spatter. It gave Sam an idea.

"You may be able to help me," Sam said. "You think you can talk to the local coroner? See if you can get any details?"

"Sam, may I remind you that the reason we are here is my sister's wedding. That is my priority."

"I know. I know," Sam said. "I just figured you could use a little break now and then."

She shook her head, knowing full well what he was doing.

"You know you want to," he teased.

Carla rolled her eyes. "I'll do what I can," she said.

"Of course," Sam said with a grateful smile. "Whatever you can do."

"But you've got to do your part, too," Carla replied. "We've got lunch with Nessa and Ray tomorrow. Then the rehearsal, then the rehearsal dinner, then the wedding. And you need to be there for all of that. Got it?"

Sam nodded.

"Our wedding was so much easier," he said.

"Our wedding was officiated by an Elvis impersonator," Carla replied, referring to their rushed Vegas wedding.

"I know," Sam said. "It couldn't have been more perfect."

Carla giggled and kissed her husband on the forehead.

"I've got to get dressed," she said.

"Don't mind me," Sam said, pulling up a chair to watch the show.

Carla laughed again, grabbing her clothes, and returning to the bathroom for privacy.

"Hey, here's a question for you," Sam spoke loudly

so she could hear him. "How long does it take someone
to bleed out from a slit throat?"

"Depends," Carla answered. "If you hit the carotid
artery, it's quick. You'd be unconscious in seconds, dead
a few minutes after."

Unconscious in seconds, Sam thought. *If the killer
struck fast, that would explain no sign of struggle. But who
would Frank let stand behind him so they could grab the
knife?*

He needed to talk to Charlotte.

18

BY THE TIME Sam returned to the house, the media cluster in front of the home had grown to about a dozen reporters and camera operators. Not enough to pose a huge problem but enough to be annoying. Per Gilford's instructions, Sam had the Uber driver take him around back where he was let in at a small gate near the garage entrance.

Inside the house, a cleaning crew was already hard at work removing all the blood in the office.

So much for preserving the crime scene, Sam thought.

Sam was led back to the library where Gilford and William were huddled in a hushed conversation. They both stood when they saw him.

"Everything okay?" Gilford asked, referring to Sam's sudden departure earlier.

"Police chief just needed to mark his territory," Sam replied, then turned to William. "I need to speak to your mother."

Both William and Gilford took a step forward.

"Why?" they both asked, almost in unison.

Sam smirked. "Jinx. Y'all owe each other a Coke."

William shook his head in disbelief.

"Relax. Just gathering information," Sam said. "She was the first to see the body, so I want to talk to her before she loses it all. Don't worry. Your turn will come."

"You don't really think one of us did it, do you?" William asked.

"I'm just gathering information," Sam assured. "Now... your mother?"

Charlotte was sitting on a bench in the backyard garden, staring at the stepped waterfall that fed into a large koi pond. A million thoughts, worries, fears and memories flooded her mind and stirred into a painful blend of aching and loss. Frank had been the center of her world for all of her adult life. Like all couples, they had their ups and downs, but their love was always strong. He had always been there, and she had never even considered that he wouldn't be. And now, just like that, he was gone.

Why? Why would he kill himself? she thought.

She began to second guess everything she had ever

done. Signs she must have missed. Triggers she might have pushed. She felt guilt and sadness... and rage.

How could he do this to me?

Then, just as quickly, the rage was extinguished by a flood of guilt for even having such a thought. And then it all started all over again.

Still, none of it felt real. She fully expected to hear his loud laugh booming from the kitchen at any moment.

"Mrs. Cannon?" Sam asked gently as he approached.

To her it was just a muffled noise, so she was startled when she finally noticed a man standing beside her.

"Mrs. Cannon, I'm really sorry, but I need to ask you a few questions while everything is still fresh. Is that alright?"

Charlotte nodded gently and Sam sat down next to her.

"How are you doing?" he asked. "Can I get you anything?"

She smiled weakly and shook her head. Sam had learned that it's best to slowly pull a grieving person out of their thoughts.

"That's a great pond," he said. "I bet you spend a lot of time out here."

She nodded, but still said nothing.

"Did Frank like it?" he asked.

She sucked in a breath at the mention of his name, but then nodded again.

"He seldom took the time to just sit and relax," she said, her voice barely a whisper. "But after a bad day, he'd sit right here to decompress. Sometimes I'd join him, but most of the time I gave him his space. Now, I'm wishing I would have spent more time with him. I just thought..."

Her voice trailed off as her mind wandered. Then she forced herself back into the conversation.

"Thank God all of my kids are here. I can't imagine being alone right now."

"Mrs. Cannon, I -"

"Please, call me Charlotte."

"Charlotte, I know this is really hard and I hate to have to do this, but I need you to tell me everything you can remember about last night and this morning."

"Are those reporters still out front?" she asked.

"That didn't take long, did it? I bet news is spreading all over town. And rumors will soon follow. Was it really a suicide? Was it a cover-up? Did he get caught having an affair? It breaks my heart just thinking about it."

"Hopefully, I can help put a stop to all of that," Sam said. "Whatever the truth may be, I'll find it and that will at least stop the rumors."

An amused smirk cracked across Charlotte's face.

"Rumors have no regard for the truth," she said.

Sam nodded, giving Charlotte time. She finally spoke.

"Last night was wonderful," she said. "It's rare that we're all together at the same time. Even at the holidays, someone is always traveling or visiting the other side of their family."

She laughed as she recalled the evening.

"I was over the moon as any mother would be. But Frank was in heaven. He loved his family so much. We kept stealing glances at each other and smiling. We knew exactly what the other was feeling. I'm so grateful I have that memory."

She explained how she had presumptively had a big dinner prepared to keep everyone in the house.

"I know my kids," she said. "A good meal is the one thing none of them can resist. And it was a great meal. A feast. Food. Wine. Lots of wine."

"I know William was already pretty drunk when they all dropped me off."

Charlotte sighed.

"Do you have any children, Mr. Lawson?" she asked.

"I have a son," Sam said. "About Peter's age."

Sam felt guilty claiming the child that he had barely ever seen, much less raised. When Sam was a young police officer in Houston, he had it all. A great job, a wonderful wife and a healthy baby boy, Nick. But the pressures of the job soon led to long hours and heavy drinking. His wife eventually left him, and Sam never did much to reach out to his estranged son. Partly out of guilt but mainly because he didn't feel he had anything to offer. After he began to clean up his act a few years prior, he had reached out to Nick, who was now living in California with a wife and young son of his own. Their reunion didn't go well and, after unleashing years of justified resentment, Nick had asked Sam to leave his family alone.

"Then you understand," Charlotte said, jolting Sam back to the present moment. "You forgive in your child what you would never excuse in others. William has been going through a lot lately."

Sam nodded, not feeling qualified to respond.

"I'm assuming it's all work related," Charlotte continued. "He's not one to share and I don't want to push it. Being a parent to adult children is a tightrope, as you know."

Sam felt increasingly uncomfortable talking about parenthood, so he waited a respectful minute as he tried to think of a tactful way to get back on track.

"Back to last night... Donny stayed, too?"

He immediately realized it was less tactful than he had hoped, but Charlotte didn't seem to notice.

"Donny always stayed," she replied. "I'm aware that may seem odd and, to be honest, I know it's uncomfortable for Rebecca, which makes it awkward for me. But Frank still feels like Donny is one of his sons. He's been William's best friend since grade school and always a part of the family, long before he and Rebecca were married. After their divorce, Frank made it clear that Donny was still a part of the family, whether Rebecca wanted to be married to him or not."

"Wow. That had to piss Rebecca off," Sam said.

"Oh, there was a big rift for a while," Charlotte replied. "Rebecca wouldn't speak to her father. But eventually, she resigned herself to it."

"So back to last night," Sam said. "You all had dinner."

Charlotte nodded and smiled as she recalled the evening.

"It was such a wonderful evening. And, because everyone had been drinking, I forbade any of them to drive. I fully expected William and Julia to walk home, but they were all having such fun everyone wound up staying the night. I was absolutely elated. I was already planning a big breakfast."

Her voice cracked as the reality of day returned. Sam switched topics again, afraid he was losing her.

"The police told me the security system was turned on at 11:10 p.m.. Does that sound right?"

Charlotte nodded.

"Yes. I remember because I had forgotten to set it and had to get out of bed."

"Did you always set the alarm?"

"Frank hated that security system. He always claimed that he forgot to set it, but I think he didn't do it on purpose. So, I just took it on as my responsibility."

"So, you set the alarm and went right back to bed?" Sam asked.

"Not right to bed," she replied. "I could hear everyone in the dining room laughing and talking, so I sat at the foot of the stairs and listened for a while. I couldn't make out what they were saying, but I didn't care. Just to hear all my children enjoying each other's company was music to my ears."

"Can I ask you a few questions about this morning?" Sam asked.

But before she could answer, her phone pinged. As she read the text, her shoulders dropped.

"And it begins," she sighed. "It's a reporter wanting a statement."

She stood up, letting Sam know the interview was over. "I really need to try and contain this, but if you have other questions, you can come back later today."

Before Sam could respond, Charlotte was walking away.

19

SAM HAD LOOKED around for any of the Cannon children, but they had all gone on with their day.

So much for staying put, Sam thought.

Instead, he decided to visit Frank's office at the dealership. He still found it strange that Frank's home office was so void of any paperwork or laptop. Even if he had just gone in there to kill himself, there would be some signs of work. Papers. Files. A computer. Anything. But the desk was completely bare. Maybe Frank was just compulsively neat. A look at his work office would solve that riddle.

Sam took another Uber to the Cannon Autos dealership on the outskirts of town. Like most car dealerships, it was a sprawling parking lot of shiny cars, trucks and SUVs. Sam entered the showroom, surprised to find the doors open.

You'd think the owner's death would be enough to close up for the day, Sam thought.

Inside, it was immaculate and spacious, housing several cars and several more giant images of Frank with his arms spread wide. If Sam hadn't actually met the man, he would have cynically written off Frank's beaming smile as the fake charm of an egomaniacal car salesmen. But Frank's grin was genuine, and Sam had no doubt that the man in the posters really was beckoning him to enter.

Sam walked through the showroom. There were a few salespeople all huddled together, no doubt whispering about Frank's death and probably also wondering why they were open. He beelined it to a receptionist desk near the back of the showroom which served as the gateway to where Sam assumed Frank's office was located. The young redhead behind the desk was deep in a conversation on the landline. It sounded like she was trying to calm an upset customer.

"I understand... You're completely right. That makes no... Let me transfer you to someone in service who can... I promise I won't keep you on hold. If you'll just let me...."

Walking confidently, like it was just another day at the office, Sam breezed past her. She glanced at him, and Sam made a conspiratorial eye roll, as if he understood her pain, then walked through the large glass door.

He walked down the hallway, checking the name plates outside of each office as he went. Expecting Frank's office to be the grand room at the end of the hallway, he was surprised to see it nestled in the center of all the other small offices. It was pretty standard, as offices went. The hallway wall and office door were glass, preventing any privacy. The office itself consisted mainly of an L-shaped desk flush against one wall. A horizontal filing cabinet ran along the back wall, under a window looking out over the sales lot of cars. The bland eggshell-colored walls were bare except for a couple of car posters. There was nothing on the desk, other than two framed photos. One of Frank and Charlotte on vacation. And one of the entire family that was at least ten years old.

And a laptop.

So much for someone stealing it.

Sam jumped as the high-pitched buzz of a circular saw pierced the air. He turned to see a small construction crew cutting and hanging sheets of drywall in new offices being built across the hall. He coughed from the drywall dust lingering in the air and shut Frank's glass door to block out as much as possible.

He walked behind the desk to rifle through the

folders stacked in a filing rack on a side desk. Above it was a single shelf that held owner's manuals and sales brochures. Sam sat in Frank's leather chair, the only sign of extravagance in the room. He traced his fingers across the desk, leaving a trail in the thin film of white drywall dust that covered just about everything.

Everything except the laptop.

He carefully lifted the laptop by its edge, being careful not to smear any potential fingerprints. The area underneath the laptop was covered in dust.

Sam opened the office door and approached the construction workers operating the saw.

"Excuse me," he yelled over the loud buzzing.

The saw's shrill buzzing wound down until it fell silent.

"What time did y'all start working this morning?" Sam asked.

"I don't know," the worker said. "About five? We try to get as much work done as possible before they open."

"Was anybody here when you got here?"

The worker shook his head with a shrug.

"If there was, I didn't see 'em."

He yelled back to his crew and asked the same question. They all shook their heads.

"What time did the salespeople start showing up?"

"Not until the past couple of hours."

"Did you see anybody in this office?" Sam asked, pointing back to Frank's office.

"Lots of people been going in and out of there all day."

"Is that typical?"

"Oh yeah. It's like a train station. They're always getting files out of the cabinets. Especially when the boss man isn't here. I haven't seen him today."

Sam didn't have the heart to tell them why the boss man was late. He thanked them for their time and walked back into Frank's office, sitting down behind the desk and staring at the clean laptop.

Someone had only recently put that laptop in here. And it couldn't have been Frank.

His thoughts were interrupted by William.

"What the hell are you doing in my dad's office?" he asked as he stormed into the room. "Get out of his chair right now."

"Just trying to understand your father better," Sam said as he rose from the chair. "I'm surprised to see you here today."

"Business doesn't take the day off," William snapped. "And someone's got to captain the ship."

"Looks like you jumped right into that role," Sam observed.

"You think I want to be doing this right now? You

have no idea how many fires I need to put out," William seethed. "Trust me. It's a role I could do without."

He jumped as the sound of the circular saw shook the room.

"Well, the sooner we talk, the sooner you can get back to your fires," Sam yelled.

William shut his eyes in resignation and nodded, yelling back to Sam. "Let's go to my office where it's not so loud."

20

WILLIAM'S OFFICE was closer to what Sam had figured Frank's office would look like. The large corner space had a couch and a cherry wood desk that was both impressive and imposing. Sam felt sure that's exactly what William intended.

"Did you and your dad get along?" Sam asked as they both sat down.

William ignored Sam, signing a few papers and moving around some files. It was an obvious power move, but it only made Sam laugh.

"People want to believe we didn't get along, that I was jealous, that my dad was... disappointed," William said. "Yeah. I've heard all the things people say. But there's nothing further from the truth. We got along great. There was nothing but mutual respect between us."

Having seen the dynamic between the two men just one day earlier, Sam knew that wasn't entirely true. But he let William go on.

"He was the showman. And I was the businessman. He sold cars. I diversified our business holdings. He did car commercials. I led our expansion efforts into ten different states. I mean, beyond the actual selling of cars, this company's success is all me. And Donny."

"Tell me about that," Sam said. "Your sister divorces a guy, but then you not only make him the CFO, you also keep him in the family. Does he do Christmas with all of y'all?"

William shrugged.

"He was my friend way before my sister snatched him up. And he was CFO before they got divorced," he said. "Just because she gets all flaky doesn't mean we all have to suffer. Donny's a good guy. And a helluva money whiz. You wouldn't know it from looking at him, but his mind is a human calculator. It's crazy. My dad put him in complete control of the business's finances and, let me tell you, our overhead has dropped, and our net profits have soared. Donny runs a tight ship. My dad would even joke that he couldn't get a can of soda from the vending machine without checking in with Donny first."

"What's your relationship with your sister?" Sam asked, switching gears. "And your brother?"

"We get along great," William said without hesitation. "I mean, there's the usual sibling squabbles, but nothing bad."

"What about your father?" Sam asked. "How was his relationship with them?"

William thought about his answer.

"Honestly? I don't think it was that good. I mean, he loved them. But he saw them differently than he saw me. He never took Rebecca seriously as a businessperson or even a salesperson, against my advisement, mind you. I always told him that with the right mentoring, she could be great. And Peter... well, Dad just saw him as the spoiled baby of the family."

"What about your mom?" Sam asked. "How does she see all of you?"

William smiled.

"Come on. She's a mom. She adores us," he said. "Honestly, I don't think we could do wrong in her eyes."

"God bless moms, right?" Sam replied.

"I'll drink to that."

"Speaking of which," Sam said. "I heard you had quite a bit to drink last night."

William bristled.

"I had a good time. Sue me," William said. "I wasn't obnoxious or anything. And I wasn't driving."

"You had to stay over," Sam said.

William shrugged. "Seemed silly to walk home that late when there's a perfectly good empty bed right there."

"Where did you sleep?" Sam asked. "Which room?"

"My old bedroom. Upstairs at the opposite end of the hall from my parents."

"And you didn't hear anything?"

William shook his head.

"I already told the police this. I'm a heavy sleeper. Ask my wife. A tornado could have blown through the house, and I wouldn't have heard it."

"And you didn't get up at all in the night? To take a leak? Throw up? When I used to drink a lot, I'd have to get up all night long."

William grinned.

"Like I said, I sleep hard. Now is there anything else you want to know, or can I get back to business?"

"Do you know anyone who would want to kill your dad?" Sam asked.

The blunt question stunned William. Sam could see him thinking about his answer.

"Well, you seem to think it was someone in the house, so what you're really asking me is if anyone in my family would want to kill him. And the answer to that is an easy 'no.' Aside from the fact that we all loved him, let's face it, Dad was everyone's meal ticket. I'm sure they're all panicked now, wondering if they'll have to go get a job."

"Or they're overcome with grief because they lost someone they loved," Sam offered.

"You don't think I'm sad?" William snapped. "We all grieve in our own way, Mr. Lawson. And right now, I don't have time to be sad. I need to keep dad's business running. And I think you need to leave."

Sam shrugged as he stood.

"Do you know who all have been in the office today?" he asked.

William was visibly annoyed by the question.

"How the hell would I know?" he said. "I just got here."

"Do you have a sign-in sheet? Or security cameras?"

"No. Cameras aren't operational right now because of the expansion" William said. "You can ask Vicki at the reception desk about who's been here today. On your way out."

21

WHILE SAM WAS SEARCHING for clues at the car
dealership, Peter Cannon was sifting through the
garbage bin behind the family home. Using a large stick
he had found, he pushed the garbage around, gagging
at the smell.

"Boy, the homeless around here keep getting uglier
and uglier," Julia commented, shocking Peter.

She had decided to take a break in the backyard
when she had seen someone lurking near the bins.
When she realized it was Peter, she decided to sneak up
on him. From how he had jumped when she spoke, she
had clearly succeeded.

"Jesus, what the hell?" he yelled.

"I could ask the same of you," Julia said. "What are
you doing?"

Peter looked at the trash bins and searched for a good answer.

"I can't find my phone charger," he finally said. "I think Mom threw it out."

Julia wasn't buying it. Peter would just as soon buy a replacement before looking for something that was missing. He threw his trust fund money around as if it would last forever. William had often said that if anyone were to go broke in the family, it would be his entitled younger brother.

"You know your parents have an entire junk drawer full of phone charger cables, right?"

"Yeah. I..." Peter fumbled. "I checked. I couldn't find the kind I needed. You know how they keep changing the type of charger inputs on the phone?"

"Oh. What kind of phone do you have?" Julia asked, trying to trip him up.

Peter could smell the trap. If there were spare chargers for the type of phone he had, he'd have to stop looking. Why did Julia even care?

Julia had been a part of the family as long as Peter could remember. She and William met their freshmen year of college and got married shortly after graduation. They never had children, much to William's disappointment. Julia was unable and William was unwilling to adopt. He wanted a true bloodline or nothing. It remained a sore subject. Luckily, no other siblings had any children either. Although Peter looked forward to that day, just so he could see the pained look in his older brother's face. He didn't have a strong feeling about Julia one way or another. She was nice enough and tended to keep more to herself than everyone else did. So why was she being so curious now?

"Honestly, I don't even know," he said with a smile. "But the charger was brand new. It was one of those high-speed chargers. I don't want to lose it."

"You need some help?" Julia asked, knowing full well he wouldn't accept it.

"Thanks. No sense two of us smelling like trash."

"Fair enough," Julia said.

The two shared an awkward moment as Peter waited for her to leave him alone. She finally broke the silence.

"Hey, can I ask you a nosy question?"

"You can ask," Peter replied.

"Is it true your dad was going to stop your allowance?"

The question hit Peter like a baseball bat. Julia wasn't sure if he was surprised that she would ask about it or shocked with the news itself.

"Of course not," Peter said weakly, faking a laugh. "Where'd you hear something stupid like that?"

Julia shrugged.

"Just what I heard."

"Heard from who?" Peter asked. "And for your information, it's not an allowance. It's my trust fund. I don't need it. I have a job, unlike some people."

"Oh, that's right," Julia said, smiling. "How is your job? Party planning, right?"

"It's event consulting," Peter replied. "And it's going great, thank you.

"Event consulting. Sorry. I forget what they call drug dealers these days."

Peter smiled. He saw the game Julia was playing.

"Hey, how's your horse doing?" he asked.

The question threw Julia. Frank had gifted William and Julia a young thoroughbred the previous Christmas.

"What's his name again?" Peter continued. "Blaze Up?"

"Blaze of Folly," Julia said, clearly not fond of the name. "Your father had already named him for us. Thought it was funny. And he's doing fine."

"Race him yet? I hear you spend a lot of time at the stables."

Peter flashed his wicked grin to make it clear he was insinuating something else. Julia grew flush.

"He's not ready yet. There's a lot of training. I like to stay involved. It's fascinating."

Peter grinned. "I bet it is. All that riding."

"Good luck with your treasure hunt," Julia said, changing the subject back. "I'll keep an eye out in the house."

"Thanks, Julia. You're the best," Peter said, not even trying to hide his insincerity.

22

THE POLICE OFFICER opened the morgue door for Carla
and yelled into the empty room.

"Jerome! You've got a visitor!"

Carla nodded at him in appreciation. She was
dressed professionally in black slacks, white blouse,
and a gray blazer she had borrowed from her sister.
And even though she was far out of her jurisdiction, she
wore her ME badge on a lanyard around her neck. Her
hair was pulled back tight into a bun - a practice she
began years ago as a way to be taken more seriously. As
a female medical examiner in the good ol' boys'
network of the police department, she needed to play
every card she had to get respect.

"Jerome! You in here?" the officer yelled again.

"Hang on!" a young female voice yelled back.

Carla heard the loud scrape of a metal chair sliding on the floor followed by footsteps coming in their direction. A young woman with long, dark hair pulled back in a ponytail appeared from around a corner, still wiping the corner of her mouth. Carla guessed that she couldn't have been older than her mid-twenties.

"Sorry," the woman said. "You caught me having lunch."

"Jerome, this is Dr. Davenport. She's an ME from Texas. Wanted to see how we do things up north."

The young woman beamed and extended her hand.

"Dr. Davenport! Welcome to Saratoga. I'm Deputy Coroner Mallory Jerome. So nice to meet you."

Carla smiled back at the young coroner.

"I'm sorry to interrupt your lunch," she said. "I'm in town for a wedding, and, frankly, I got bored looking at flowers. I'm kind of a morgue nerd."

"Ha! I get it," Mallory said. "I've been to so many weddings this summer, I may get physically ill if I see another dress with a giant bow on it."

Assured that they were okay, the officer said goodbye and shut the door behind him.

"You're having lunch awfully late," Carla said. "Are you that busy?"

"It's been quite the week," Mallory replied. "And I get stuck with the paperwork. Rookie duties, you know."

"It will get better, I promise," Carla said.

"I don't really mind," Mallory corrected with a laugh. "It's a great way to learn."

"Good for you," Carla replied. "We need more women in this field. Are you here alone?"

"For a while," Mallory said. "My boss is in a meeting. Playing politics."

"Trust me. You're much better off down here," Carla said.

"So, did you want a tour or something?" Mallory asked.

"I'd love one! But I don't want to impose."

Mallory laughed.

"My clients can wait," she said, throwing in some gallows humor that Carla appreciated..

She walked Carla through the L-shaped morgue.

"Not much to see. Wall of drawers over there. Couple of examining tables here. Offices are in the very back."

"Working on anything interesting lately?" Carla casually asked as she looked around.

"Check this out," Mallory said.

She walked over to the walled compartment and slid out a metal drawer. A sheet covered what was obviously a corpse.

"It's not murder or anything," she said. "It's a

suicide. But he's kind of a local celebrity. And he slit his throat."

That's our guy, Carla thought.

"I've only seen that a few times," Carla said, walking to the other side of the covered body. "One subject used a machete. Can you imagine? What did your victim use?"

"It was a knife. Some sort of big Marine knife."

Jerome pulled back the sheet to reveal Frank's corpse. His skin was a pale gray white, except for the long crimson slash that ran from one side of his neck to the other.

"A single, long, obliquely placed, incised wound," Mallory said as professionally as possible. "Started on the left, which would indicate it was done by a right-handed person, which the deceased was. No other injuries. No defensive wounds, bruises or cuts."

"What about hesitation marks?" Carla asked.

Hesitation marks were small, parallel wounds that are typical in a suicide with a knife, caused by the victim pressing the knife against the skin while working up the nerve to do the deed.

"None," Mallory said.

"That's rare for a knife suicide," Carla said.

"I guess," Mallory said. "To be honest, it's my first one. But the cause of death had already been decided by the time I saw the body."

"What about toxicology?" Carla asked.

"Full reports won't be back for a week, but preliminary work showed a high blood alcohol level. Nothing out of line with someone having a few drinks after dinner, which his family said he had done.".

"Mind if I take a look?" Carla said.

"Be my guest," Mallory said. "Why? You see something?"

Carla took her blazer off and slipped on a pair of latex gloves. She leaned down to get a closer look at the throat.

"Not really," she said. "I just haven't seen very many of these. Guns are pretty much the weapon of choice in Texas."

She ran her finger just above the laceration.

"The depth of the laceration is kind of odd for a suicide, don't you think?" she asked.

Mallory leaned in.

"What do you mean?"

"Well, he was sitting at his desk," Carla said as she straightened up and pantomimed someone sitting at a desk. "He'd grab the knife and probably look straight ahead while he..."

She acted out slitting her own throat.

"It would start deep and get shallower as the arm pulled away. But this incision is the opposite."

Mallory examined the injury again.

"I didn't even notice that," she said. "But if someone was standing behind him..."

Mallory made the motion with her right hand to mimic if she was slitting someone else's throat. Carla nodded.

"Exactly."

Carla examined the scalp to see if there was any sign of hair being yanked out.

"I examined the head and the hair," Mallory said. "Nothing abnormal at all."

Carla sighed. "Which makes our little murder theory unlikely to stand up in court."

"Still, should I add the observation to the notes?" Mallory asked.

"You could," Carla said. "But it's a bold claim that would no doubt get a lot of scrutiny. I don't know if you want that."

"Well, we have to tell the truth."

Carla admired the young coroner's integrity.

"I'd add it to the notes. But just the part about the depth of the laceration being uneven," Carla advised. "Second-guessing a detective can get tricky. Although they technically aren't the ones who should be calling a cause of death."

"Oh, my boss did that," Mallory replied. "He was at the scene. I've just been doing all the formalities."

Carla smiled.

"All the more reason not to second-guess the cause of death," she said. "Just write something like 'the laceration appears to grow more shallow as it cuts horizontally, typically not seen in a suicide'. Leave it at that."

Mallory nodded, satisfied with that compromise. Carla was glad Mallory wasn't going to push it. From what Sam had told her, she would be throwing fuel on a fire that no one wanted to burn. Still, including the observation in the official report could keep things from coming back to bite Mallory if it became a murder case.

She asked if she could do a more thorough examination, promising not to disturb anything.

Sam's right, she thought. *This is not an open and shut suicide.*

23

SAM HAD his Uber drop him off a few blocks from his hotel. It was a beautiful late afternoon and Sam wanted some time to process everything he'd learned so far. He didn't realize that a stroll through downtown Saratoga Springs would have so many distractions it would be next to impossible to focus on anything. The people-watching alone was overwhelming.

Sam mistakenly assumed all the tourists were at the track. But the streets were crowded with a lot of people apparently not interested in gambling. There were lots of frazzled young parents trying to keep up with their energetic kids. Elderly couples walking hand in hand. Other people walking their dogs. There were a lot of dogs. People were sitting at outdoor cafes or seeking shade at one of the many open-air bars. Others were trying to handle more shopping bags than one person had a right to carry. Sam passed a cigar shop, where a group of men lounged in leather chairs calmly watching the frenzy all around them. He paused, inhaling the sweet aroma, and was tempted to join them.

As he turned into Congress Park, he noticed a round white structure surrounded by young families. He soon understood why. The structure housed an old-fashioned carousel where little kids rode wooden horses in a circle while a pipe organ played carnival music. But Sam had another destination in mind. The hotel concierge had told Sam and Carla that a couple of the town's many famous mineral springs was located in the park and Sam wanted to give it a try.

He walked along a small stream that ran through the center of the park. Ducks were either swimming in it or foraging around it, looking for food from generous picnic-goers. He looked around at the statues and fountains that decorated the park until he saw what the concierge at his hotel had shown him. A Greek pavilion made up of a green roof and several white columns. In the middle was a cylindrical fountain with water pouring out of four spouts all around it. It was Congress Springs - one of the town's many famous mineral springs that were not only the town's namesake, but what put the town on the map. They attracted rich and powerful people from all over the world. In fact, according to the concierge, George Washington himself visited the town after the Revolutionary War. More than a century later, FDR visited the springs to see if they could help his health problems.

Sam watched people filling large plastic jugs and small plastic cups with the water that poured out of the center structure. Realizing he wasn't properly equipped, he wondered how to get his hands on a cup.

"You can use your hands," a young woman said.

Sam watched as the woman walked up to the fountain and cupped her hands under the water then drank from them. Sam nodded, a little hesitant.

"What does it taste like?" he asked.

"Just remember, you're not drinking it for the taste," she said. "It's for the healing properties in it."

Sam stepped up to a spout and filled his cupped hands with the spring water, bracing for the worst as he drank it. It took him by surprise.

"It's a little fizzy," he said, grimacing as he took another sip. "Kind of salty."

He stepped back, his curiosity satisfied.

"Every spring is a little different," the woman said. "This one is supposed to help upset stomachs."

"I'll stick with Pepto-Bismol," Sam said.

The young woman laughed.

"Can't beat the healing powers of neon pink," she said, extending her hand. "My name's Natalie. Natalie Edgars."

24

SAM INTRODUCED himself to the young woman and thanked her for her help.

"I couldn't visit Saratoga Springs without actually drinking from a Saratoga spring," he said.

'Where are you visiting from?" she asked. "I can tell it's the south."

"Wrong," he said with a smile. "I'm from Texas."

He turned to walk up through the park toward his hotel, but Natalie followed.

"So, what brings you to Saratoga?" she asked, immediately realizing she was sounding suspiciously curious. "Sorry. I get a kick out of learning why tourists come to town."

"My wife's sister is getting married," he replied.

"You look so familiar to me," she said.

Sam waited for her to make the connection to the true crime documentary, enjoying his celebrity moment. He was not expecting her follow-up.

"Weren't you at the Cannon house earlier today?"

He turned to study her more closely. He should have seen it. The young, earnest eyes. The nervousness in her conversation.

"You're a reporter," he said.

"Look, I'm just curious," she said. "I just saw you leave with that officer this morning and I didn't recognize you. And you're visiting from Texas? Something's going on, right?"

Sam laughed.

"Sorry to disappoint. I'm an old friend of the Cannons. I was even at the track with them yesterday. This morning, I got a call from William and rushed over to see if I could do anything to help them."

"Why did you leave with the police? And how did Frank Cannon seem yesterday?"

"Okay, thanks for the water advice, but I've got to go."

"You know I'm going to find out who you really are," she said. "Why not just tell me the truth now?"

"Why can't you leave a grieving family alone? Look. I get it. I've dealt with young reporters like you my whole career. You're wanting to make your name. Nab a big headline. But I've seen it backfire a million times. Be careful. Know the full truth of what you're talking about before you turn it into news. Because if you have to take it back later, your career is as good as over."

"So, why don't you tell me truth?" she asked. "Protect me from myself."

"Frank Cannon sadly died by suicide this morning," Sam said. "The family is grieving and so am I. Please leave us all alone."

Sam walked away, praying the young woman wasn't following. But her words stuck with him.

You know I'm going to find out who you really are.

And she would. He had stupidly given her his real name before he realized who she was. Thanks to that stupid documentary, his name would pop up right away on a Google search. He sighed and decided to just lean into it.

"And you know, I'm a private detective," he said as he turned around. "But that's just a coincidence. I'm in town with my wife for a wedding. And I'm a friend of the Cannon family. That is it. And if you plan on speculating beyond that, be prepared to be sued. Whether I win it or not won't matter, it will be enough for you to lose your job."

Natalie nodded. Sam could tell her mind was spinning with what she should do next. He decided to leave before she came to any conclusion.

She seems smart, he thought. *Hopefully, she'll do the smart thing.*

25

S AM WALKED into the large open room of the restaurant, surprised to find it so busy. All the high-top tables and booths were filled, but there were still a few stools at the massive bar. It ran the entire length of the room and seemed stocked with every libation imaginable.

Sam walked through the tables to a man sitting at the bar. The man was engrossed in the day's horse races, which were being broadcast on the bar's TV. Sam sidled up beside him.

"I figured you'd be at work like William," Sam said to Donny.

Donny looked at Sam with a smile, not even surprised to see him.

"I don't know how that robot can work today," he said.

From his slurred speech, it was apparent he'd been at the bar for quite a while.

"Some people would probably say the same thing about a guy watching the races."

Donny smirked.

"Just something to do while I drink."

Sam was surprised that Donny didn't ask how he had found him. He was actually quite proud of his sleuthing, so he decided to tell him anyway.

"Your family owns this bar," Sam offered, answering a question that wasn't asked. "So, I'm guessing drinks are free."

Donny laughed.

"My EX-family," he corrected. "And we don't drink the profits. Hell, if we did that, we'd have gone broke years ago."

"Frank was like a dad to you, wasn't he?" Sam asked.

"I know what you've got to be thinking," Donny said, motioning to the bartender to get him another drink and one for Sam.

Sam thought about asking the bartender for a water. He knew that when he drank, he sometimes didn't know when to quit. Most of the time, that had led to a lot of bad decisions, bar fights or trips to the city jail. He had promised himself — and Carla — that he would behave himself while he was in Saratoga. But he also knew that a drinker like Donny would be suspicious of a non-drinker and Sam needed him to put his guard down. One drink would be alright.

"I'm the nightmare ex that won't leave," Donny continued.

Sam laughed. "I've already been briefed on the situation. You and William go back forever, and Frank still sees you as family."

"Yadda yadda yadda," Donny interrupted. "And before you ask, it's not weird for me. I mean, it was at first, but the only one that's weirded out about me being around is Rebecca. And I kind of enjoy that."

"So, who called it quits?" Sam asked. "If you don't mind me asking."

"That's what detectives do, right?" Donny replied. "I thought things were good between us. Then one day out of the blue, she just announced she didn't want to be married anymore. Couldn't be held down. No other explanation than that."

"Another man?"

Donny shook his head. "That's what I thought. But if there was, he never surfaced."

"So, you're an insider but also an outsider," Sam said. "That gives you a unique point of view."

"How do you mean?"

"You've got a better sense of the dynamic in that family," Sam said. "I mean, things are tense now, but that's normal after someone in the family dies. You know what it's like normally."

The bartender brought over two glasses of whiskey on the rocks. The two men clinked glasses and Donny took a hard gulp. Sam pretended to drink more than he did and set his drink down where it wasn't as visible to Donny.

"That family is a powder keg," Donny said. "They all pretend to get along but there is no love lost between William, Becca, and Peter. Frank doted on them, but you could tell he didn't really have any respect for any of them."

"Even William?" Sam asked.

"Look. I love William. He's like a brother. But he can't hide his ambition and that bugged the shit out of Frank. He still saw him as his little kid. Hell, he still saw me as the little neighbor kid. But I just keep my head down and do my job. It frustrated the hell out of William."

Donny glanced at Sam.

"Don't get me wrong, though," he said. "I don't think anyone in that family has the stomach to kill anyone."

"What about Charlotte?" Sam asked.

26

SAM'S QUESTION caught Donny by surprise.

Donny stopped to think, then shook his head.

"Nah. No way. Not Mrs. Cannon. She's one of the kindest, most sincere people I know."

"You'd be surprised what people can hide from others," Sam said. "I've seen a lot of perfect marriages wind up with one dead spouse."

Donny laughed.

"I believe that. But not Mrs. Cannon. No way."

"So, tell me about last night," Sam said, quickly shifting gears again.

Sam had tried to tell himself it was his interrogation style. Quickly changing subjects, asking random questions, anything that helped throw the subject off - even for a second. It gave him a glimpse at the real person, not the one they're trying to pretend to be. Truth be told, it was just the random way Sam's mind worked.

"What about last night?" Donny asked.

"Walk me through it," Sam said. "After y'all dropped me off, you all went back to the house."

"Yeah, William had invited me to dinner."

"Was that normal?" Sam asked.

"Totally. Like I told you, whether Rebecca likes it or not, everyone else still considers me family."

Donny walked Sam through the photo shoot, and then dinner.

"Dinner itself was pretty low-key," Donny recalled. "Lots of 'how was your day?' small talk. Mainly, everyone focused on the food to avoid conversation. Towards the end of dinner, things started loosening up."

"Not that it was a drunk fest," Donny said, waving his finger. "Except for William. He got a little out of hand."

"How so?"

"William's a mean drunk. He was picking fights, spilling drinks. Everyone tried to ignore him. Julia, bless her heart, had to keep calming him down."

"He fight with anyone in particular?" Sam asked.

"Well, Peter was being his usual asshole self, so he brought on a lot of it. Honestly, William was just calling him out on his bullshit the way the rest of us wanted to."

"How was everyone else acting?"

Donny shrugged.

"Rebecca just kept shaking her head and rolling her eyes at her brothers fighting. Julia, like I said, kept trying to make peace. So was Charlotte. Frank was laughing. It was all just harmless 'boys being boys' shit to him."

"What about you?"

Donny smiled.

"I have learned through the years to stay out of William's line of vision when he gets like that," Donny said. "Actually, most of the time when I'm with the family, I try not to engage too much. Probably why they like me so much. Last night, I just settled back and watched the show. Unfortunately, that meant I did more drinking than I wanted to, which is why I wound up passing out on the couch."

27

WILLIAM PULLED into the long driveway of his palatial Victorian home. It was the second largest house in the North Broadway neighborhood, second only to the Cannon estate where William grew up and which was only a block away on the other side of the street. The home's light gray cedarwood siding was accentuated by white shutters that framed each of the twenty windows facing the road. It was a massive house, much larger than a couple with no children could ever need. But William didn't buy it for practical reasons.

He sighed as he got out of his silver SUV, spotting Julia's black Escalade near the garage. He had hoped she would be out somewhere, maybe still at his parents' house. He just wanted to pour a glass of bourbon and attempt to process all that had transpired in the past twelve hours. But when the front door was unlocked, he knew she must be home.

"Julia!" he yelled. "You here?"

There was no response.

But before he could look for her, he was distracted by the sound of a car pulling into the driveway. William looked out a window to see a blue Porsche Boxster come to a stop. In seconds, there was a knock at the door.

"Shit," William muttered under his breath.

He opened the door to a nervous Rebecca.

"Hi, William," she said, letting herself in.

She was dressed in black leggings and an old Journey T-shirt. Her hair was tangled, and she obviously hadn't bothered to clean up the mascara that had ran down her face from a day of crying.

"Where were you all day?" she asked.

"I was at the office," William seethed. "I told everyone where I was going."

"Were you in there shredding secret documents?" Rebecca asked, only half joking.

William just rolled his eyes.

"What are you doing here, Becca?"

Rebecca walked into the living room and sat down on the couch.

"Please," William deadpanned. "Have a seat."

"I need to talk to you about something," she said.

William could see she was serious. He sat down in a chair across from her.

"What's up?" he asked.

Rebecca fidgeted in her seat.

"Before he... before last night, did Dad talk to you about me?" she asked.

William was confused.

"You'll have to be more specific."

Rebecca took a deep breath, mustering up the courage to say something.

"Last night, Dad pulled me into the kitchen to tell me that he was going to make me the marketing director for the company."

She looked at William to see if he already knew, but he remained stone-faced.

"He did, huh?" William asked.

"He said he already talked to you about it, and it was all set up."

A bead of sweat formed on William's forehead.

"He said that?"

Rebecca nodded.

"He didn't give me any of the particulars, and with everything that's happened today, I didn't know what I needed to do next."

"Rebecca. Jesus. You think this is the time?"

"He did talk to you about it, though? Right?"

William looked into his sister's eyes, mulling over his response.

"Did he?" she asked again.

"Rebecca. I'm sorry," William finally said.

Rebecca's shoulder dropped in disappointment. She shook her head.

"I knew you'd lie about it," she muttered.

"I swear. This is the first I'm hearing about this," William said.

Tears filled Rebecca's eyes again as she glared at William.

"I'm not saying he didn't say all that to you," William said. "But you know how Dad is. Maybe he was going to say something to me."

"He said the two of you had already made arrangements," Rebecca said. "Why would he say that if it weren't true?"

William shrugged.

"Maybe he thought he had? Maybe he was going to? I don't know what to say, Becca."

"Well, now you know," Rebecca said. "So how do we do this?"

William struggled for the right words.

"This may not be the right time for something like that," he said.

"You piece of shit," Rebecca said.

"Come on," William said. "Dad just died. That's

going to cause all kinds of ripples through the company. It's just not a good time to do something like this."

"But you will do it," she said. "Right?"

"Sure," William said.

Rebecca could tell he was lying.

"Right. I see," she said, her anger beginning to boil. "You want the business all to yourself."

"No," William argued. "It's not like that. There's just a lot to deal with right now."

Rebecca rolled her eyes as she stood up.

"Oh, poor you," Rebecca snapped.

"You have no idea what kind of responsibility I have to live with," William said.

"Give me a break," Rebecca said. "That job is the only thing you care about. For all I know, you killed Dad so you could have it all for yourself."

"I want you to leave," William growled.

"That detective said it had to be someone in the house. You sure had the most to gain."

"What is wrong with you?" William scowled.

"We've all heard you complain about how Dad is the only thing holding you back," she continued.

William stood up, clenching his fists.

"You need to leave."

"Calm down," a woman's voice said. "Both of you."

Julia, wearing a silk-cashmere track suit and wet

hair, had come down the stairs. She quickly moved between the two siblings.

But William was too riled up. He stepped closer to Rebecca, yelling into her face.

"You've been complaining about being under his thumb your whole pathetic life."

"He was my dad!" Rebecca yelled.

She began to break down, burying her face in her hands. Julia motioned for William to stand down as she pulled Rebecca into her arms. Rebecca crumbled in grief. But just as quickly, a bolt of rage shot through her and she pushed away, turning on William once again.

"He's dead because of you!"

Julia tried to calm her down, but Rebecca shook her off, ready to fight.

"Alright, both of you!" Julia yelled, clearly fed up. "Stop this. Now!"

It was enough to stun the siblings into silence.

"What are you doing?" she continued. "Try being a family for once. Even if it's just for your mom's sake."

William nodded, looking down at the ground in shame. But Rebecca was still burning hot. She stared at Julia, shaking her head.

"Of course you're going to side with him," she said calmly to Julia. "Anything to help your man get ahead. You benefit if he does, right?"

Julia slapped Rebecca hard across the face.

"You're grieving and you're lashing out. I think you need to go home," she said, using every ounce of self-control to hold in her anger. "Now."

Rebecca glared at her sister-in-law as she rubbed her red cheek. The slap seemed to snuff out her fury, but she was still smoldering. Without saying another word, she left, slamming the door behind her.

28

SAM AND DONNY stayed at the bar, watching the long day dissolve into evening. Sam had managed to avoid drinking, discreetly pouring his drinks out in the spill tray of the bar. Even though Donny was oblivious, the bartender had caught on and had been playing along with the charade. Sam figured he probably had seen other people do the same thing. Besides, what did he care? He was getting paid either way.

Over time, the conversation had steered away from Frank's death and on to other things, like the horse races.

"How often do you go to the track?"

"It's a short season here," Donny answered. "So, we try to go as often as we can."

"And by 'we,' you're referring to the Cannons?"

Donny nodded, but his smile quickly faded.

"I wonder how that will change now," Donny said. "Frank was the only other one that really loved the track. We'd have to drag William and Gilford along. Without Frank..."

Donny finished his drink and the two men sat in silence. Sam turned to look around the restaurant. It had somehow gotten even more crowded than when he arrived. It was a broad mix of people, just like the track. In fact, Sam guessed that many of these people had been at the track and had left early to beat the dinner rush in town. As he scanned the crowd, he noticed a man standing outside, looking at him through one of the large front windows. He was thin, probably in his late 40s. With dark, tousled hair, a five-o-clock shadow and deep brooding eyes. When he saw Sam looking back at him, he quickly glanced down and walked away. Sam didn't think much of it. Other people walked by and looked in the window, probably deciding whether it was worth stopping in. He turned back around to face the bar.

"How often does Frank's horse run?" Sam asked. "You said Frank had a horse, right?"

"Yeah. Cannonball Run," Donny said with a fond smile. "And then there's Julia's horse, which was really Frank's."

"How often does Cannonball Run race?" Sam asked.

Donny shrugged. "A few times here each season. But he races at other tracks, too. Frank used to travel with him a lot, but work has been so crazy lately, he hadn't had the time."

"Is he good?"

"He's solid," Donny said with a grin. "Pays his share of the rent. Now Julia's colt... that's the one to watch. Only two years old and has got some impressive speed. One more year and he'll be old enough to run in the Travers."

"Travers?"

"It's a stakes race here in Saratoga. Has a nice payout," Donny explained. "A big deal. And Blaze has a good shot at it."

He slapped Sam on the shoulder.

"And that's an insider tip for next year. Don't forget. Blaze of Folly."

Donny struggled off the barstool, suddenly aware of how much he had had to drink.

"Good thing I walked here," he said.

"You live up by the others?"

Donny laughed.

"Not on your life," he said. "That's a waste of money. Especially for a single guy. I've got a really nice town-home a couple of blocks from here. You'll have to come by sometime. I've got a pool table in the basement. Fully stocked bar. We can grill some steaks."

"Sounds nice."

"Open invitation, buddy," Donny said. "Food's good here. You should get something. Put it on my tab. Along with your drinks."

He turned toward the exit of the restaurant. The place had filled up since he had arrived, so he needed to find the best way to maneuver his way out without bumping someone's table.

Sam watched Donny wind his way through the crowd, stopping to greet several people along the way. When he walked out the door, Sam turned back to the bar.

"Get you another?" the bartender asked as he walked over. "Or maybe a water?"

"A water would be great," Sam said with relief.

"No charge for the water," he said. "Your other drinks are on Donny's tab."

"He must be quite the regular to have a tab," Sam said.

He reached for his wallet and pulled out a twenty.

"Does he normally come alone?" Sam asked, putting the tip on the counter.

"Most of the time. Sometimes with friends. Sometimes with a date. A lot of them pour their drinks out, too."

"Same woman every time?"

The bartender laughed. "You're awfully interested in his business."

Sam laughed back as he stood. "Sorry. Ex-cop. Force of habit. You have a good night."

"Thanks," the bartender said, picking up the twenty-dollar bill. "And it's different women."

Sam nodded in appreciation and turned to find his own way out of the restaurant. As he looked out the window, something caught his attention. It was the mystery man from earlier, standing across the street, looking toward the restaurant.

Sam pushed through the crowd, finally making it to the door. By the time he made it outside, the man was gone. Sam looked around, but there was no sign of him in any direction. Deciding he was being paranoid, Sam shook it off with a laugh and headed up Phila Street toward his hotel.

29

THAT NIGHT, Sam and Carla had a late dinner at one of the hotel restaurants, a popular farm-to-table steakhouse. Normally, it would have been next to impossible to get a reservation, but Carla's soon-to-be brother-in-law knew the owner and was able to wrangle a table for two for them while he and Vanessa endured dinner with his family at an Italian restaurant down the street.

Sam was starving and looking forward to a steak dinner. He didn't even protest when Carla told him to dress up a bit.

"Nothing fancy," she had said. "You can wear jeans, but just wear a blazer."

Sam hated jackets in the summer as much as he hated ties. Two throwback fashion choices that had no place in summer wear. But if it meant a juicy ribeye, he would have worn a tuxedo.

Aside from the promise of red meat, Sam also wanted to treat Carla to a nice night out. He felt guilty that he was starting to get consumed by the case. Actually, Carla was relieved he had something to do while she dealt with her sister's wedding preparation. Truth be told, she'd much rather be working with him on a murder investigation than coordinating floral deliveries.

Not realizing this, Sam put extra effort into asking questions about the upcoming wedding – even appearing interested when she answered. He was proud of himself and was sure he was depositing a lot of brownie points into his new husband bank. But she finally had enough.

She took a sip of wine and sat back, crossing her arms.

"I can't believe you're not even going to ask me," she said.

Sam searched for the question he was supposed to know, but he was baffled. He went through a mental checklist. The wedding. Her sister. The fiancé. The search for a venue. Carla could see the panicked look in his face.

"You'll be glad to know that I was able to sneak away for a bit and visit the coroner's office," she said.

Sam sat up. Why hadn't she mentioned this earlier? She was probably waiting for him to ask. Now he felt foolish. He figured she would get mad at him for bringing up work. But maybe it was a trap. He decided to play it cool and shrugged nonchalantly.

"Great," he said. "I mean, if you want to talk about the case."

"Do you know me, Sam Lawson?" she grinned. "I get what you're doing, and I really appreciate it, but we both know what we both would rather be talking about."

Sam smiled at his wife, falling in love with her just a little bit more.

"Something is definitely off," Carla continued, getting serious. "To start with, the entire report, including the cause of death, was rushed. Secondly, there were a lot of things left off the report."

She told Sam about the discrepancy in the depth of the incision.

She grabbed a butter knife and a roll to better explain.

"With a suicide, the depth of the wound would start deep and slowly get shallower as it moves laterally."

She held the dinner roll up to her neck and cut into it from left to right.

"It's physics. As your hand moves closer to your arm,

you can't apply the same amount of pressure," she explained. "But in Mr. Cannon's case, the incision was reverse. It grew deeper as it moved laterally."

"What would cause that?" Sam asked.

"One possibility is that the one with the knife was standing behind the victim."

She held the roll lower and cut through it to demonstrate.

"So, he WAS murdered," Sam said.

"It's just a theory," she admitted. "And there are a lot of other factors at play. The length of the knife handle. The length of the victim's arms. His shoulder strength. Without doing a full analysis, I can't make any definitive conclusions."

"But is it enough to get the police to take a second look at the cause of death?" Sam asked.

"Typically, I'd say yes," Carla said. "But the deputy coroner had been instructed to leave the body alone, so she's hesitant to bring it up with her boss."

Sam nodded.

"Maybe this will be enough for Durant to open his eyes," he said.

"Hopefully," Carla said.

Sam nodded and calmed himself down.

"This is great," he said. "I can't believe you were just sitting there with all this information without saying anything."

She shrugged coyly.

"I knew you weren't going anywhere."

30

SAM STARTED the next day with a full agenda. He needed to share Carla's findings with Detective Durant and convince him this case wasn't as open and shut as he wanted it to be. He also still needed to speak to several members of the family. And, on top of that, he had to juggle it all with the growing wedding obligations he had promised Carla he would not miss, starting with meeting his sister-in-law and her fiancé for breakfast.

To thank Sam and Carla for making the trip, Vanessa and Ray had insisted on treating them to breakfast at the racetrack. Every morning, the racetrack opens up the porch of the Clubhouse to the public. It was at ground level and right next to the track, so you could watch the horses train while you dined.

"I hate that Ray missed this," Vanessa said as they were finishing the meal. "But I guess that's the real estate business for you. When a client needs you, you must respond, or you could lose the sale to someone else. He has promised he will make it up at lunch."

Sam tried to hide a sigh. He had forgotten that they were also supposed to have lunch with the couple today. He fueled up with coffee, while Carla and Vanessa sampled the racetrack's signature drink: the Saratoga Sunrise.

"Mmmm," Carla said. "What's in this?"

"I think it's orange juice, vodka and green something," Vanessa replied.

"Grenadine," a waiter interrupted with a smile. "Do you like it?"

"I love it," Vanessa said. "I may love it too much. Do not let me order a second."

"It does go down easy, though," Carla said with a laugh. "You want to try it, Sam?"

Sam shook his head.

"I'm gonna stick with coffee, thank you," he laughed.

Sam found himself enjoying the breakfast. Vanessa was always good company, and he did enjoy watching the horses.

But his mind kept wandering back to the Cannon case and he started getting antsy. Maybe, since Vanessa's fiancé had opted out for a work-related emergency, Sam could do the same. He had made it through the meal and it's not like he was contributing much to the after-breakfast conversation. The two sisters were so lost in childhood reminiscences, they wouldn't even notice he was gone. He decided to take a chance.

"Ladies, I hate to break this up, but I really need to get going.""You made other plans?" Vanessa asked.

"It's a case," Carla offered, trying to help Sam out.

"You took a job?" Vanessa asked. "While you're here for my wedding?"

"It just kind of happened," Sam replied meekly.

"He has sworn that he will not let it interfere with your big day," Carla chimed in. "Right, Sam?"

"I swear," he replied. "I waited until after we ate."

From the look on both women's faces, he immediately knew that was not the right thing to say.

"You two don't need me right now," he rationalized. "And I want to get a jump on this now, so I can have it done before lunch today."

"You are not missing lunch," Carla said.

"I swear on Texas," Sam replied, hand on his heart.

"What's the case?" Vanessa asked. "Anything good?"

Sam hesitated.

"I'm not at liberty to discuss it," Sam said sheepishly. "Police orders."

"The police are involved, too?" Vanessa asked. "This

must be good. Is it about that suicide? I heard it was gruesome."

"He'll tell you about it at lunch," Carla interjected. "Right, Sam?"

Sam stood, realizing Carla was graciously giving him his exit.

"I will tell you all that I can," Sam said. "I promise."

Vanessa grinned mischievously.

"Oooh, I hope it's juicy," she said, clearly no longer annoyed.

Sam leaned down and kissed Carla.

"Thank you," he said quietly.

31

SAM WALKED out of the clubhouse gate and headed toward Union Avenue. It was a nice morning, and he could use the thinking time as he walked back downtown. Union Avenue was a wide boulevard lined with large trees and divided by a beautiful median filled with colorful flowers. However, Sam barely had a chance to appreciate the scenery. He was distracted by a woman driving past him in a black Escalade. It was Julia Cannon.

Sam hung back so he wouldn't be seen and watched as Julia drove into a driveway directly across the street from the track's main entrance. Sam dodged traffic as he ran across Union to follow her. He saw her car parked on the other side of a gate marked AUTHORIZED PERSONNEL ONLY that was guarded by security. Then he spotted her walking toward several rows of small buildings.

He looked at the security gate. There was no way he was going to just waltz in.

Fortune was on his side that morning, though. A garbage truck pulled into the lot and stopped at the gate, giving Sam enough time to run to the far side of the truck then, using the truck as a shield, walk beside it as it slowly drove past the security gate. When it picked up speed, Sam jumped on a side rail, startling a garbage worker who was also riding the side of the truck.

"You can't be here," the garbage worker yelled.

Sam put his finger to his lips and quickly flashed his Texas PI badge. The piece of metal was enough to satisfy the garbage worker, who nodded in puzzlement. As the truck drove into the rows of low buildings, Sam couldn't help but notice all the horses.

These are stables, he thought. *Julia is just coming to see her horse.*

He spotted her walking down a dirt track between two rows of stables and he saluted the dumbfounded garbage worker as he jumped off the truck. Out of the corner of his eye, he was pretty sure the garbage worker saluted back.

Sam slinked down the same dirt path as Julia, being sure to keep a safe distance between them so he wouldn't be noticed. Luckily, the horses provided ample cover. Trainers, doctors, and jockeys were all milling about, tending to different horses. Sam walked through confidently, looking like he belonged. He even grabbed a stray clipboard that was sitting on a bale of hay.

A clipboard always makes you look like you're working, he thought.

When Julia stopped in front of a small building, Sam stopped, too. Hiding behind a horse, he pretended to check things off an imaginary list as he watched Julia knocking on a door.

The horse blocked a lot of his view, but he could make out that someone had opened the door and Julia was speaking to them. Sam tried to get a better look, but the person never emerged from the doorway and the horse wasn't letting Sam move too far. He was able to see Julia looking around nervously as she pulled an envelope from her purse and handed it to the person in the doorway. He watched the person check the contents of the envelope, then saw Julia smile and nod before stepping into the open doorway, shutting it behind her.

Sam walked around the horse to see if there was any kind of sign on the door but just as he got close to it, Julia emerged. Sam spun around and walked back in the opposite direction. He weaved through a few horses and then ducked into an empty stall.

He watched as Julia walked away and, once he was

satisfied, she was out of sight, he headed back toward the door she had visited.

"Hey! What are you doing?" a voice yelled out.

Sam turned to see a security guard walking quickly behind him.

"You can't be in here!"

There was no way for Sam to escape, so he didn't run. He thought about flashing his PI badge, but then he'd be on record for being there and he didn't want Julia to find out he had been following her. Instead, he discreetly set the clipboard down, put on a confused expression and walked toward the guard.

"Oh, thank God," Sam said. "I am so lost."

"How'd you even get in here?"

"I don't know. I don't even know where I'm at!" Sam said, acting like a confused tourist. "Dang GPS must have got me off course. I'm looking for the track."

"That's on the other side of the road, mister," the guard replied.

He grabbed Sam's arm and guided him back toward the gate.

"How did you get past security?" the guard asked.

"Beats me," Sam said. "I was looking down at my phone, trying to figure out where I was and next thing I knew, I was here. I knew it didn't look right, but I saw the horses, so I figured I was close. I'm in from out of town and meeting my wife and her sister for breakfast at the track. That's a thing, right? To be honest, I was only half listening. I'm so late. They're going to be furious with me."

Sam's rambling was enough to convince the guard he was just a confused tourist.

"I'll take you over there," the guard said. "See if your story checks out."

32

"This man says he's supposed to be meeting you here," the security guard said to a shocked Vanessa and Carla.

But Carla knew Sam well enough to know what he'd done.

"There you are!" she said as she stood up and hugged Sam, turning to Vanessa and making an expression urging her to play along as well. "See? I told you he'd make it."

Vanessa was confused, but she quickly caught on. "I owe you five bucks, Sis. He made it."

Sam apologized for being late, explaining that he had gotten lost on the other side of the track. Satisfied that he really was just another lost tourist, the security guard let him go and wished them a good day. But not without issuing a stern warning to Sam first.

"When you're walking around, pull your head out of your phone for a second and look at the street signs," he said. "Particularly pay attention to signs that say DO NOT ENTER."

Sam nodded and thanked the security guard for helping him, then he sat down with the two women again.

"Sorry about that," he said.

Vanessa was giddy.

"Oh, that was fun," she giggled. "Is this what life with you two is always like?"

"More than you want to know," Carla said.

Sam explained where he'd been, but without naming any names. Not in front of Vanessa.

"So, what are you going to do now?" Vanessa asked.

"I need to talk to Detective Durant," he said.

Thirty minutes later, Detective Durant's silver Chevy Malibu pulled up to the clubhouse gate to pick up a waiting Sam.

"I got your text. You've got fifteen minutes," Durant said before Sam had even settled in his seat.

"That's it? No 'Good morning?' 'How's your day?' or 'Gee. You look really nice. Is that a new shirt?'"

"Cut the crap," Durant said, unamused. He pulled a

U-turn and then headed north on Nelson Avenue. "I'm heading to the station. You have until we get there to talk."

Sam wasted no time. He began to share everything he had learned, beginning with the suspicious relocation of the clean laptop.

"That's reaching," Durant said. "There was no sign of the laptop at the house and there's a million reasons why the laptop was cleaner than the desk."

"Okay. Well, get this. My wife is a medical examiner in Texas," Sam said.

"She sounds too smart for you."

"She went to the morgue and looked at Frank's body."

"Damnit, Sam!" Durant snapped. "That's crossing the line."

"And she noticed something odd," Sam continued. "The slash across Frank's throat was at an odd angle for a self-inflicted wound. But the perfect angle for someone grabbing him from behind."

Durant thought about it for a second, then shook his head.

"That's conjecture. It's a very loose theory at best."

"What about this?" Sam tried again. "Not even thirty minutes ago, I spotted Julia Cannon delivering an envelope of cash to a stranger in the stables."

"What do you mean a stranger?" Durant asked.

"I mean, it was mysterious circumstances," Sam said.

"Who'd she give the money to?"

"I couldn't see his face."

"But you know it was a man?"

Sam stammered. "I'm pretty sure it was."

Durant laughed. "You know she owns a racehorse, right? That means she has a trainer. She rents a stable. She has to buy food. There's a veterinarian. There are all kinds of people she could be paying. Come on, Sam. You're wasting my time."

Durant pulled into the police parking lot, not saying a word.

"I know any one of these things on its own is nothing," Sam said. "But there's a lot of it. At least enough to warrant taking a second look."

Durant smirked. Sam started to offer another argument, but Durant held up his hand. He seemed to be thinking as they drove in silence the rest of the way to the police station. They even got out of the car in silence until Durant finally spoke.

"You've got a lot of half-baked ideas that can all be easily explained away," Durant finally said. "And it's not a lot. You gave me three flimsy things. Sorry, Sam. I can't do anything with any of that."

Sam groaned.

"Come on," he said. "I can tell you're a smart cop.

You know sometimes the truth isn't right out in the open."

"And sometimes it is," Durant argued. "No matter how hard you don't want to believe it."

"I'm not giving up," Sam said.

"That's why they're paying you," Durant replied.

He turned to leave but stopped, turning back around.

"I'm not being stubborn to be stubborn. If you can prove me wrong, I will admit it," Durant said. "But you've got to prove it."

Sam nodded and watched as Durant walked toward the police station. It was just after nine o'clock and there was still so much Sam needed to do. He felt exhausted just at the thought of navigating it all on foot or by Uber. He pulled out his phone and dialed a number.

"Gilford? he said. "It's Sam. You think you can get me a car?"

33

GILFORD HAD someone pick Sam up and take him to the car dealership, where Gilford and a black 2020 Ford Fiesta were waiting for him.

"This is one of the loaner cars," Gilford said. "I've arranged for you to have it for a few days."

Sam smiled. It was perfect for getting around and blending in.

"I really appreciate this," Sam said.

"If it helps you figure out what happened any sooner, then it's worth it," Gilford replied.

Sam had barely driven off the lot before his phone rang. He didn't recognize the number, but it was another 518 area code.

"Hello?" he answered.

"Sam Lawson?" a vaguely familiar female voice asked.

"Who's this?"

"Natalie Edgars. We met in the park yesterday."

Sam let out a sigh. *How did she get his number so quickly?*

"Both of our jobs require a little bit of detective work," she said, seeming to read his mind. "So, you're kind of a famous detective."

That damn documentary.

"Not that famous," he grumbled.

"What? You don't like being a mini celebrity?"

"What do you want, Miss Edgars?" Sam asked.

Per Natalie's directions, Sam drove about ten miles east of town and pulled into the apple orchard parking lot. He walked across the gravel lot to the small, open-air building where baskets of fresh produce and assorted apples were on display. In the back, a few people were ordering coffee and pastries at a counter. Sam walked through the store towards another open door that led outside to a cluster of tables. That's where the young reporter was waiting for him.

"So, what's so important you couldn't share it over the phone?" he asked as he sat down.

"I just need you to confirm a few things," she said.

"And you want to be able to see my reaction," Sam said. "I know your little tricks."

He could tell Natalie was nervous. She clearly was still a little wet behind the ears.

"I wanted to meet out here so we could be discreet," she said. "Like you asked."

Sam nodded in resignation.

"What do you want to know?" he asked.

"I saw the coroner's report," she said.

"How the hell did you see that?" Sam asked.

"I have friends that work at the morgue," she said. "I noticed something odd."

"I haven't seen the report, so I can't help you," Sam said. "Sorry."

"The report noted that the location and angle of the incision was different than what you would typically expect from a self-inflicted wound," Natalie said. "Is that true?"

They both studied each other as if they were in a high stakes poker game.

"I don't know," Sam finally said. "He was still a bloody mess when I saw him."

"So, you saw the body?" Natalie asked.

She fought back a 'gotcha' smile.

"Be careful," he finally said. "Remember what I said about reporting speculations."

"If you tell me what's going on, I won't report it now," she said. "As long as you keep me in the loop."

Sam smiled.

"I used to know a reporter like you," he said. "Young and ambitious to a fault."

"Yeah?" Natalie asked. "What happened to her?"

Sam sighed. "She got her own TV show."

He leaned forward.

"Look, all I know is that the family and the police ruled it suicide," he said. "I have no reason to believe differently."

"I think you're lying," she said. "I think you believe it was murder and you're looking for the killer."

"I think you watch too many true crime documentaries," Sam said. "But let's say I am, which I'm not. You go reporting something like that, it might scare the killer away. He'd high tail it out of town before we could ever prove it. Would you want to be responsible for that? Letting a killer go free? Would you want to be known for that? Because I would make sure everyone knew you did it knowingly."

Natalie thought about what Sam said.

"This story could be the break I've been waiting for," she said.

"It's not a story," Sam said. "It's a person's life. A good reporter knows the difference."

Sam could see the wind blow out of her sails and he actually felt a little sorry for her.

"How about this? If I hear anything, I'll give you the

scoop," he said. "But only if you keep a lid on it for now."

Natalie nodded cautiously.

"Don't screw me over, Mr. Lawson," she said.

Sam grinned as he stood.

"You have my word," he said. "But don't get your hopes up about any of this. I don't think there's a story here for you."

34

HAVING a car definitely had its perks, but it also had a few disadvantages. When Sam returned to town, he found himself slowed down by traffic and a seemingly never-ending search for parking. Finally giving up, he used the valet at his hotel, knowing he would pay through the nose for that luxury. But he figured he could bill it to Gilford. Besides, he had a lunch appointment that he had promised he wouldn't miss.

"So sorry I'm late," Sam stammered as he scrambled to the table.

He had got there just as the waiter was placing glasses of water on the table.

"There's the man," Ray said, standing to shake Sam's hand.

"I'm really sorry," Sam mumbled softly. "I was looking for parking."

"I can definitely relate to that," Ray laughed. "And hey, you made it. That's what matters. Besides, we only sat down a couple of minutes ago."

Thank God Ray's got my back.

Sam was already liking his future brother-in-law more and more.

"They gave me a car," Sam explained. "For the case. Which is great, but I didn't account for..."

"Parking," Ray interrupted. "Yeah, it's a real problem."

"Thank you," Sam said. "I mean, not to look a gift horse in the mouth, but I was driving around for twenty minutes. I finally valeted at the hotel."

"Well, you're here now," Carla said. "You get an A for effort."

She smiled and kissed him on the cheek.

"So, they just gave you a car?" Ray asked. "What is this case?"

"He has promised to divulge everything. Right, Sam?" Vanessa said. "I mean, I lied to the cops for you, so I'm kind of an accomplice now. You owe me."

"Wait. You lied to the police?" Ray asked. "Alright. We need to back up here. I feel like I'm missing out on all the excitement."

After swearing everyone to secrecy and speaking in hushed tones, Sam filled Vanessa and Ray in on Frank Cannon's suicide/suspected murder and his own dealings with the Cannon family. He left out some of the speculative details, such as the mystery man or Julia giving money to someone. Detective Durant was right about that one. It was probably nothing and Sam didn't want to spread unnecessary gossip. He knew he had already shared enough to create a town scandal.

Sam had paused only when the waiter showed up at the table to take their orders and then again when he brought their food. The entire time, Ray just sat there with his mouth agape. Vanessa kept elbowing him, as if to say 'See? I told you Sam led an exciting life.'

"But you can't breathe a single word of this to absolutely anyone," Sam finished. "No exceptions."

"So, Frank Cannon was murdered?" Ray finally asked. "Holy crap."

"Officially, it's being treated as a suicide" Sam corrected. "

"But you're not so sure about that," Ray said.

"I've been hired to exhaust all possibilities," Sam said diplomatically.

"Oh, that doesn't sound suspicious at all," Ray said with a laugh.

"Did you know the Cannons?" Sam asked.

Vanessa chimed in. "Oh, Ray knows pretty much everyone in Saratoga."

Sam looked at Ray for confirmation and the real estate man nodded.

"Oh, yeah," Ray said. "Hard not to know that family. They're a pretty big deal around here. I mean, everyone knows Frank because of his commercials. But pretty much the whole family is a big part of the social scene here. Big philanthropists. Always hosting charity events. Big supporters of the hospital, the library, museums, and SPAC."

"Spack?" Sam asked.

"Saratoga Performing Arts Center. SPAC," Ray explained. "It's a big outdoor concert spot. A lot of big-name acts."

"In two weeks, we've got tickets for the Zac Brown Band," Vanessa added. "Second row."

"So, you know OF the family, but do you know them?" Sam asked, trying to keep the focus on the Cannons.

Ray nodded. "Hell, I went to school with William and Rebecca. I mean, we weren't great friends, but we hung out off and on. Then we all went off to different colleges. They both got married. I got into real estate. I did sell Rebecca and her then husband their first house."

"Donny Stanton," Sam said.

"Right," Ray said. "I forgot you already met everyone."

"What can you tell me about them?" Sam asked. "Anything of interest?"

Ray drummed his fingers on the table as he thought.

"Not really," he said. "William's been kicked out of his share of restaurants and bars. He's a big drinker. But they all seem like good enough people. William has fed me some business through the years. Rebecca and Donny are super nice. Rebecca is really involved with a lot of the charities. She and her mother. And Julia, William's wife.

He laughed. "The men make the money, and the women give it away, right?"

Sam flinched. Even he knew that was not going to land well with Carla and Vanessa. Ray immediately realized the same thing.

"I'm joking," he said. "Bad joke. Stupid thing to say."

"What about Peter?" Sam asked, trying to quickly change the subject in an effort to save Ray.

"Peter," Ray replied, not sure whether to answer Sam or apologize more to the two women. "I don't know much about Peter."

"Nothing?" Sam asked again. "Anything at all?"

"Look, I'm really sorry about that joke," Ray said,

understandably more concerned about digging himself out of the hole he had dug. "It was stupid of me."

Vanessa patted his shoulder and smiled.

"At least you know your place," she said. "You make it. I spend it. Got it?"

Ray couldn't tell if she was joking or not, but knew his only choice was to nod.

"Ray. What about Peter?" Sam asked again.

Ray shook his head.

"He was younger. Plus, he moved away so... out of sight, out of mind, right? But I do know he's kind of the black sheep of the family. Always getting in trouble. Bar fights. Public intoxication. I think he got caught selling drugs. But that could just be a rumor."

"He sounds like a real peach," Carla said. "Okay. Enough murder talk. We have some wedding details to work out."

"Oh, this is way more exciting," Ray said, once again realizing he had stuck his foot in his mouth. "That's not what I meant."

Sam shook his head to signal to Ray to stop talking.

"Look, I have one request," he said, hoping to distract the conversation.

"We know," Carla said. "Pigs in a blanket and chicken wings."

"Oh, I love pigs in a blanket," Ray said, turning to Vanessa. "We're doing that, right honey?"

"We'll look into it," Vanessa said, kissing Ray on the cheek. "In the meantime, you should probably just stop talking."

35

DETECTIVE DURANT STARED at his blank computer monitor lost in thought and oblivious to the frenzied pace of the police station. As much as he just wanted to dismiss what Lawson had told him, it was bothering him. What if he had been hasty in his investigation? When dispatch contacted him, they had described it as a suicide. Had he gone in with preconceived notions? He knew better than that.

He gave himself all kinds of excuses. He had only slept a few hours, up most of the night investigating other crimes. He was spread thin and had already been dreading the mountain of paperwork waiting for him. Had he subconsciously wanted to avoid adding to the pile?

He replayed the events of that morning. Arriving at

the house. Surveying the home office. Examining the body and talking to the coroner who had beat him there. Even the family kept referring to it as suicide. Everyone except their lawyer, but Durant wrote that off to denial. He'd seen it a thousand times.

It wasn't that Lawson's findings contradicted anything Durant had done. It was flimsy hearsay and prejudiced conjecture. Still, it planted a seed.

What if? Durant thought.

It was the question that helped make him a good detective. But had he asked it that morning? He could honestly say he hadn't. It looked cut-and-dried, and he was more than happy about that. But did that frame of mind cause him to miss something?

He typed in his login credentials and searched for the case file, poring over it to see if there was anything he missed. The only possible thing that stood out was that he hadn't followed up with the home security company to double-check the time of activation and de-activation.

He looked up the security company's number and called. He had made these types of routine follow-up calls hundreds of times, and they had always been a waste of time, which is likely why he skipped it. But doing it now would at least give him the peace of mind that he had dotted his i's and crossed his t's.

After navigating through the automated prompts,

he finally reached a human. He introduced himself, gave his badge number and asked for the system details for the night in question. As per protocol, the security company would have to fax the information to the station versus tell him over the phone. Durant thanked the security agent and hung up.

About fifteen minutes later, Durant heard the fax machine humming and buzzing. He made his way over to it, stopping to refill his coffee cup along the way, and arrived just as it was spitting out the report.

As he walked back to his desk, he casually skimmed over the report. What he read caught him completely off guard.

36

DONNY KNOCKED on the door frame of William's office as he walked in.

"Hey there," he said.

William peered up from a stack of papers with a total look of desperation.

"Holy crap," Donny said. "Guess I won't be asking 'how's it going?'."

He plopped down in one of the chairs facing William's desk.

"I swear to God," William said. "Between my work and my dad's, plus all the phone calls I now have to field, I'm buried."

"So, your dad did more work than you thought, huh?" Donny asked.

"I guess so."

"How can I help?" Donny asked.

"Remind me that I love my job," William replied.

"You love your job, William."

"Bite me," William replied.

"But seriously, how ARE you doing?" Donny asked. "I mean, aside from the work crap."

"I don't even know," William answered. "I haven't even had a chance to process any of it. It's like I'm on autopilot. I'm not eating. Not sleeping. I'm not even drinking."

"Whoa, this is serious," Donny teased.

William put his head in his hands.

"I'm in way over my head, Donny."

"Come on, man. You were made for this shit."

William shook his head. Self-doubt and anxiety were getting the best of him.

"I don't know. I don't know. It's just too much."

Donny got up and walked around to William's side of the table.

"Come on," he said. "You need to get out of here. This can wait."

"It can't!" William protested.

"It can and it will. You're going to have a breakdown if you don't step away for a minute. And then you'll be sidelined even longer."

"The board is asking a lot of questions," William argued.

"Your dad died. They're going to have to wait for their answers. Come on. I'm driving you home."

"Can we go to my mom's house instead? I need to check in on her."

"You don't need to do everything," Donny said as he guided his friend out of the office. "But a little Mom Time may be good for you."

37

Durant barged into Chief Morelli's office.

"You need to see this," he said, shoving the security report in the chief's face.

"Whoa, slow down," Morelli said, taking the fax from Durant. "What am I even looking at?

"It's the activity log from the Cannon's home security system on the night of Mr. Cannon's death.

"That's a closed case, Durant," Morelli said, pushing the report to the other side of the desk.

"I know, but I just wanted to double-check a few things and realized we'd never run an activity log. I thought I was just doing some due diligence but look. Right there."

He pushed the report back to Morelli and pointed to a line on the document.

"The system was turned off at 1:05 a.m. and then re-activated at 4:12 a.m.," Durant said. "We assumed no one broke into the house because it would have set off the security system, but someone turned it off for three hours."

Morelli looked at Durant, waiting for the detective to give him more.

"That changes everything," Durant said.

"I'm not sure how," Morelli said, once again giving the fax back to Durant.

"Three hours is more than enough time for someone to come in, kill Mr. Cannon, cover their tracks and then leave," Durant explained. "Plus, it fits the time of death perfectly. We need to re-open the case."

"You realize that the official cause of death has been released," Morelli said. "It's been on the news. Hell, it made national news. You now want to go on the record that you made a mistake? With all the other problems this department's been dealing with?"

"Maybe we did make a mistake," Durant said.

"Maybe YOU made a mistake," Morelli replied. "You were acting detective. This was your case. I'm not being a jerk to be a jerk. I'm protecting you now. Because I won't be able to, if you go public that you messed up."

"It's better than letting a killer walk free," Durant said.

"Whoa, whoa, whoa," Morelli said, putting up his

hands. "Don't get ahead of yourself here. Just because there's a gap in the security system doesn't mean Cannon was murdered.

"Think about it. The system was re-activated, right?" Morelli continued. "That has to be done from inside the house. And when the first officer showed up that morning, the system was on, and the family was inside. No one else. If anything, it sounds more like someone snuck out in the night and then came back. My money's on Peter Cannon. Probably left the house for a party or hook-up or Lord knows what."

"But we don't know that," Durant said.

"You want my advice?" Morelli said. "Let sleeping dogs lie. And stay away from that Texas detective. He's creating nothing but trouble."

"He's not going to just go away," Durant said.

"I'll deal with Lawson," Morelli replied. "You just need to trust me and let this go."

38

Unable, or unwilling, to sit in the dark of his family's home any longer, Peter had made a few calls then headed out to meet some friends at Saratoga Lake, stopping on the way to pick up a case of beer and a case of champagne. Max, his high school buddy and one of his oldest friends, greeted him with a hug and condolences for his loss.

"I appreciate it, but I need a break from the sadness," he declared. "This afternoon is death-free, okay?"

His friends, not comfortable dealing with heavy emotions and relieved they could party without guilt, agreed, and they all headed out on the Cannon's 24-foot luxury pontoon boat. Free from the heavy cloud hanging over his family, Peter happily escaped into the warmth of the sunny day as he sped out over the blue water.

There were already several other boats anchored in Sandy Bay, a shallow, sandy nook along the lake's southwest shore. It was the unofficial summertime hangout of Saratoga's twenty-something locals. The boats would crowd in close, sometimes tying together, to form a sun-soaked flotilla of booze, bathing suits and music.

Peter set anchor next to a lowrider filled with beautiful young women.

"Peter?" a young blonde in a tiny bikini said, clearly stunned to see him. "I'm so sorry…"

Max interrupted, making an announcement for all to hear.

"Peter is taking a break from his sadness," he yelled. "He needs friends and sunshine, not hugs and sympathy, so let's help him out, okay?"

"Well, I won't say no to hugs," Peter yelled. "As long as they are from lovely ladies."

The few people that actually listened raised their beer cans and red plastic cups in a cheer. Peter grabbed a bottle of champagne.

"Now who wants champagne?" he yelled, as he shook the bottle and popped the cork, spraying champagne into the air and all over the girls in the boat next door.

For the next two hours, Peter partied with his friends, laughing, drinking, and dancing to music blaring from large speakers on a neighboring pontoon boat. Jumping in the waist-deep water, he grabbed two women and pulled them close to him, kissing one then the other. Max pushed a paddle board toward them. It was doubling as a floating tequila bar.

"Who wants shots?" Max asked, pouring shots for all of them.

The four did shots together, followed by a victory howl.

"Good to have you back," Max yelled to Peter over the music.

"Maybe I can come back more often now," Peter said. "I'm gonna get another beer. You want another beer?"

"Have I ever turned one down?"

"Have you ever turned anything down?"

"You know me. I'll try anything five times," Max said.

Peter laughed and pulled himself back on the boat. This day was exactly what he needed. No worries. No family judgements. No dealing with all the moping and crying. His family took everything way too seriously.

They need to lighten up, he thought to himself as he grabbed a couple of beers.

As he popped the tops, he started noticing people

looking at phone screens and murmuring to each other. Then he noticed they were all glancing at him.

"What's going on?" he yelled.

When no one answered, he walked up to someone on his boat that was looking at their phone. He grabbed it out of their hands and felt his heart drop as he read the news alert that was spreading over texts.

"Shit."

39

A FEW LOCAL news vans and about a dozen reporters had already staked out spots in front of the Cannon home. Max drove past the throng as Peter ducked down in the passenger seat.

"What the hell, man?" Max mumbled.

"You can drop me off a block from here," Peter said. "I can worm my way through the back yards to get back to the house."

"You still haven't answered my question," Max said. "Is it true?"

"People are always looking for a scandal," Peter replied.

Inside the house, the rest of the family had already re-grouped in the living room. Rebecca and Julia conspired on the couch while Charlotte, William and Gilford paced nervously around the living room.

William peered out of the side of the curtains at the media and growing crowd of onlookers. If it weren't for the six-foot tall wrought iron fence keeping them on the sidewalk, they would have all been at the front door.

"How did this get out?" he snapped at Gilford. "No one was talking about murder but you."

"Scandals sell," Gilford said. "It was inevitable that someone would start rumors. That's why I hired the detective. To get ahead of it."

"Yeah, that's working out great," Peter said, walking in the back door.

"Where have you been?" his mother asked.

"I needed to blow off some steam," he answered. "But somehow Dad still managed to put a stop to that."

Charlotte looked at her youngest with pleading eyes. Peter shrugged as he plopped down in an overstuffed leather chair.

"Maybe it's just a couple of local TV stations," Rebecca suggested, ignoring her younger brother.

"It's all over social media," Peter said, mimicking a TV reporter. "This just in. Was Henry Cannon murdered? News at 11."

"So are pictures of you partying right after your father's death," Gilford said.

"How could you be so stupid?" William growled. "You're just feeding the machine."

"I'm not a robot like you, Lord William," Peter said. "I needed a break from it all or I was going to kill myself."

As he said the words, he realized how inappropriate they were. He looked down sheepishly.

"Sorry, Mom."

"You all need to stop fighting," Charlotte said. She was calm and steady, with the renewed strength of a mother whose children were threatened.

"We need to circle our wagons now," she went on. "Gilford, I need you to contact Marjorie Gutman. Tell her what's going on and have her develop a strategy."

"Your first response is to call your PR agent?" Peter asked.

"She'll craft another statement for the media," Charlotte said. "We are not to say anything to anyone, understand? Anything we say could be taken out of context and used against us."

"Are you saying I'm not capable of talking about my own father's death?" Rebecca asked. "I need to read a prepared statement?"

"It's a good idea," William interjected. "There are too many moving pieces here and we need to be very careful with what is shared."

"I think it makes us look guilty," Peter scoffed.

"In their eyes, we are already guilty," Charlotte replied. "Make no mistake about it. Those vultures out there want to crucify us. Because that's what sells. This was inevitable, just as the fact they will all move on to a new scandal in a day or two. But we can't let them destroy us in the process. Your father worked hard to give our family name a good reputation. We can easily get ahead of this by sticking together and issuing a sincere, heartfelt but carefully thought-out statement."

"Luckily, the official cause of death is still suicide, which will cut down on some of the sensationalism," Gilford said, walking to stand beside Charlotte.

"This is all your fault," William said. "If you wouldn't have hired that damn detective."

"Wait till they find out he thinks one of us is the killer," Peter said.

William nodded and turned to Gilford.

"You need to get rid of him."

40

As the family continued to alternate between bickering and plotting, something out of the corner of her eye caught Rebecca's attention. From where she was sitting, she was able to see the backyard through the kitchen window. And at the back of the expansive backyard, past the rose garden and waterfall, she could see a portion of the back fence. And at that back fence, someone was jumping up and down trying to see over it.

Her immediate thought was that it was some reporter, and she was just about to say something, but then something about the person looked familiar. She squinted to get a better look.

It's that detective, she thought.

Again, she started to let everyone know, but then she received a text.

I SEE THAT YOU CAN SEE ME. I NEED TO TALK. MEET ME OUT BACK.

Intrigued why the detective would single her out and curious as to what he wanted to talk about, she got up casually, grabbing her empty glass of water so it would seem she was just going for a refill. The charade wasn't even necessary. Everyone was so caught up in their own posturing or fixated on the growing mob out front, they didn't even notice.

When no one had answered his calls, Sam had decided to drive over to the Cannon house. The swarm of media in front of the house was larger than he had expected, and he knew it would only grow larger. He drove a few blocks away and walked back, cutting through the alley to the back of the house. But when he found the back fence gate locked, he wasn't sure how to get in. He peered through the slits of the wood paneled fence and could see the family inside. So, fresh out of any other ideas, he began to jump up and down, hoping to get someone's attention.

Luckily, Rebecca had noticed him, so he texted her. By the time she came out the back door, he was so out of breath he was growing dizzy.

"Mr. Lawson?" Rebecca asked as she got closer. She spoke in a loud whisper "Is that you?"

"Thank God," he gasped.

"What are you doing?" she asked.

"Getting your attention," he whispered back. "Can you let me in?"

"I don't know the code," Rebecca said.

"My God, can't you people just have a gate latch like the rest of us?"

"Calm down," she said. "There's another way. Follow the fence along until you get to the back of the guest house. Over there."

Sam couldn't see where she was pointing, but assumed it was at the cottage on the far side of the back fence. He trudged along the fence line, wiping the sweat from his brow as he tried to catch his breath.

"Now what?" he asked through the fence when he reached his destination.

There was no reply.

He looked between the fence panels. No one was there.

"Rebecca?" he whispered loudly.

She didn't answer.

"Crap," he grumbled.

He knew no one in the family wanted to talk to him. He should have realized she had just been distracting him so she could lose him. He leaned back against the fence, still catching his breath. Then he heard Rebecca's voice again.

"Over here," she whispered loudly.

He looked around, unsure where her voice had come from, and saw a few pieces of fence paneling swinging out and back. As he walked over, he could see that a few of the panels had been repurposed into a hidden door that swung up to allow someone to go in and out of the gate.

"William and I did this as kids so we could sneak out," she explained. "It's hidden back behind the tool shed and no one has ever noticed."

Sam marveled at the ingenuity as he slid through the fence. When she pulled it shut, he could see that ivy covered the inside of the fence, concealing the hinges that allowed the fence to move back and forth.

"What are you doing here?" she asked.

"There are still a few of you I haven't had a chance to talk to."

Rebecca sighed. "Including me."

Sam nodded. "We can do this out here or go in the house."

"Let's go into my house," she said, pointing to the guest house. "Or my 'for-right-now' house."

41

SAM FOLLOWED Rebecca through the front door of the guest house. They stepped into a spacious great room that included a restaurant-grade gourmet kitchen separated from the living area by a long grey slate-topped counter. Oak wood beams outlined the tall, vaulted ceiling, and framed a massive skylight that allowed sun to bathe the entire room. The furniture and decor looked like it had been pulled from a *Town & Country* magazine.

Sam looked around, thinking that most people he knew would be happy to call this their real house.

"They're going to fire you," she said. "Because of all the talk about murder."

"What are you talking about?" Sam asked.

"It's all over the news," she said. "That's why all those reporters are out front."

"What are they saying?"

"That Dad was murdered."

Sam was stunned. "Based on what?"

Rebecca shrugged. "Based on they heard a rumor. And there's a detective running around trying to solve a murder case."

"I have been nothing but discreet," he said, immediately regretting his conversation with Natalie.

She gave me her word, he thought.

"Well, they can fire me if they want. I'm still going to get to the bottom of this," Sam said. "If for nothing else than to shut down rumors like this."

"So even if you weren't getting paid, you'd still be a pain in the ass about all of this?" she asked.

"It's kind of my thing," Sam said with a shrug. "Something's not right about all of this and I don't like it when things don't feel right."

Rebecca thought about it for a second and then nodded in agreement.

"Can I get you something to drink," she asked, opening one of the frosted glass cabinets and pulling down a couple of glasses.

"Just water," Sam said, still taking in everything.

Rebecca put a glass under the waterspout on the black refrigerator door, then handed it to Sam.

"I'll be having something a little stronger," she said, returning to refrigerator and pulling out a bottle of white wine.

"You're really roughing it out here," Sam remarked. "How long have you had to endure this?"

"It's been eight months so far," she said. "And, trust me, living in your parents back yard is not all free rent and roses."

She led him over to the large, overstuffed white couch and plopped down, sliding one foot under her lap.

"So, what do you want from me?"

Sam sat down next to her.

"Let's start with the other night," he said. "The night of the photo shoot."

Rebecca exhaled loudly.

"We all did the dog and pony show," she said. "Pretended to be a happy, loving family for the cameras."

"But you're not that happy and loving?"

Rebecca looked at Sam sarcastically.

"You've met us, right? At best, we tolerate each other."

"What about that night?" Sam asked. "From what I've heard, you seemed to all get along."

"Honestly, I think it was the end of a long day and we were all just too tired to fight," she said. "William was his usual drunken asshole self. That can suck the life out of any room."

"What about Peter?" Sam asked.

"He likes to stir things up," she said. "He'll say things just to get a rise out of you, but instead of arguing with you, he'll just laugh in your face in that smug little way he does."

"Was there anything that happened that was out of the ordinary?" Sam asked. "Anything at all. No matter how small."

Rebecca seemed to be deciding whether to share something with him. She finally spoke.

"There was one thing," she said. "But it was probably nothing."

"That's okay," Sam said. "What?"

"Well, right before dinner I saw Dad and Julia talking in the kitchen," she said. "I couldn't hear them, but I could tell Dad was upset and Julia was on the verge of tears. And then she nodded, and he smiled, and they hugged. All very weird. I just figured something happened to her horse. Like I said, it's nothing."

"No. It's very interesting," Sam said. "That's helpful. Thanks."

Rebecca gulped the rest of her drink.

"I'm having another," she said. "Sure you don't want anything?"

"How was your father?" Sam asked. "Other than his

moment with Julia, did he seem happy? Sad? Preoccupied? Anything out of the ordinary?"

Rebecca thought about the last night she would ever get to see her father. Tears began to well up in her eyes.

"He was laughing a lot. I guess he seemed really happy. Even when we were squabbling, he would just watch us and grin."

"He seemed content?"

Rebecca looked at Sam.

"If you mean like he was appreciating it all because he knew it was about to end?" she asked. "Believe me, I thought about that. I've replayed that night over a million times. But honestly, there was nothing out of the ordinary. He was just happy. Egging everyone on, as usual. Yucking it up with the boys."

"Just the boys?"

"I'm daddy's girl," she replied. "Emphasis on the girl."

"That had to bother you."

Rebecca shrugged.

"I've gotten used to it. My time will come."

"Probably be easier now that your dad is gone," Sam said, waiting for her response.

It was a teary-eyed glare.

"I'm going to pretend you didn't say that."

Sam put up his hands in surrender.

"I didn't mean that as an accusation," he lied. "I'm sorry."

He quickly switched gears.

"What about after dinner?" he asked. "I guess it turned into a regular slumber party."

Rebecca smiled. "Yep. We all sat around a campfire and sang Kum-Ba-Yah."

Sam laughed.

"What about Donny?"

Rebecca groaned loudly.

"The mistake I can't seem to get rid of?" she asked. "He always just sits there and listens. Laughs mostly. I honestly think that's why my dad liked him so much. Personally, I think it's creepy."

Sam continued to grill her with questions. He asked how late everyone stayed up and when and where everyone went to bed. Those were questions Rebecca couldn't seem to help him with.

"I went to bed before anyone," she said. "Probably because I had this whole house to come home to. But I remember waking up around midnight and things were quiet. So, I'm guessing everyone had gone to sleep or passed out by then."

"And you were back here. By yourself," Sam asked.

"All alone," she said.

Sam's next question was interrupted by his phone's ring. He looked at the screen. Another 518 area code.

"Yeah?" he said as he answered the phone.

"Sam Lawson?" the familiar voice at the other end said. "We need to talk. Now. I'm sending you the address."

Rebecca watched as Sam hung up the phone.

"Anything important?" she asked.

Sam stood up.

"It's the Chief of Police."

42

———

Sam followed his phone's GPS to Saratoga Spa State Park, an expansive state park just south of downtown that was one of the area's most famous and historic landmarks. He drove past the impressive Lincoln Bath House, which Sam thought looked like a smaller version of the White House, then turned on to a winding road that quickly disappeared into the shade of a massive pine forest. The sun cut through the branches, creating a breathtaking tapestry of light and shadow that even impressed this boy of East Texas.

The trees eventually cleared to reveal golf course fairways and greens on either side of the road. Finally prompted to make another turn, Sam drove past a couple of parking lots and pulled into his destination, the Gideon Putnam, an historic luxury hotel and resort.

A circular driveway brought him to the front of a large red brick building accented with large white columns and rich green awnings. A uniformed valet greeted him as he pulled to a stop.

"Can I just leave the car here?" Sam asked. "Just meeting someone in the lobby. I won't be long."

"I'm sorry, sir," the middle-aged man said in a soft voice. "But we need to keep the entrance clear."

"What if I just pull over there?" Sam asked, pointing to a spot at the end of the circle.

Before the valet could speak, another voice interrupted.

"It's okay, Bobby," Chief Morelli said as he emerged from the building, his dominant eyebrows leading the way. "He's with me."

Bobby looked back at the police chief and then to Sam.

"Just not very long," he said with a forced smile.

"Scouts honor," Sam replied with a smile.

Chief Morelli patted Bobby on the shoulder as he passed him, then extended his hand to Sam.

"Mr. Lawson. Thanks for meeting me here."

"Jeez, how much do they pay cops in Saratoga?" Sam asked, looking up at the beautiful building.

Chief Morelli laughed.

"They just re-opened this year," he said. "Gorgeous

building. I'll give you a tour sometime. I'm just checking in to make sure everything's running okay."

"Wow. A police chief that makes house calls," Sam said.

"My sister-in-law works at the patio restaurant," Morelli said with a grin. "Free meal with a view."

"Is this a dinner date?" Sam asked, feigning surprise. "It's a little early."

"Calm down, Cowboy," Morelli replied. "I just wanted to talk to you away from the station."

He walked over to Sam's Fiesta and leaned back on the hood.

"I'll cut right to it. I thought I asked you not to make a lot of noise," he continued. "But all I keep hearing are complaints."

Sam was shocked. Other than the incident at the track, there had been nothing to complain about.

"I don't know what you're talking about" Sam replied. "I haven't ruffled a single feather."

"Breaking into the stables. Interfering with my coroners. And most importantly, letting your murder investigation leak."

"I had nothing to do with that last one," Sam protested. "Come on. You know how the press can be. If there's not a scandal, they're gonna create one."

The chief leaned up to look Sam directly in the eyes.

"I need you to back off," he said sternly. "Now that

things are going public, we don't need to be back-tracking."

"You'd rather let a killer go free than admit a mistake?" Sam asked.

"You've got no evidence," Morelli said. "And your theory is that someone in Frank Cannon's own family killed him. Unless you have enough evidence for me to charge any one of them, then you are hurting all of them. Oh, and even if you did have enough evidence to get an arrest, that family has the funds to lawyer up and beat any rap that isn't a straight up confession. And maybe even then."

"So, you're saying, let it go now because they're going to go free anyway," Sam said. "And that's what you call justice."

Morelli's face reddened and he clenched his fists.

"You know, you can stand there and be all high and mighty about justice being served, but you don't have to pick up the pieces afterwards. I live in the real world. And I've dealt with rich people like the Cannons before. In the end, they always walk away, and we pay the price. I'm not protecting them. Or myself. I have to protect my department."

"You mean, you don't want me to make you look bad," Sam interjected.

"Not just me. Detective Durant. The coroner. The list goes on," Morelli snapped back. "You're not going to take down a member of the Cannon family. You're going to hurt the reputation of good cops. Hell, you may even cost a few of them their jobs. And for what? Just to say you're right? I'm telling you. Let it go. Enjoy your vacation in our lovely city. Then go back to Texas without leaving a mess."

Sam wasn't sure how to respond. Part of him knew the police chief was right.

Morelli patted Sam on the shoulder.

"You should bring your wife here," he said as he walked away. "I can get you a discount."

Sam watched the chief walk back toward the hotel entrance.

"What if I can get hard evidence?" he yelled. "Or better yet, a confession. Something that even the Cannons couldn't beat in court?"

"Let it go, Lawson," Morelli yelled back without turning around.

Sam groaned. He opened his car door and slumped down in the driver's seat, his mind buzzing.

"Yeah, I don't see that happening," he muttered to himself as he pressed the ignition button and revved the engine.

43

KNOWING the police chief was watching, Sam drove out of sight, but then quickly pulled into the first parking lot he could find. He looked through his incoming calls to the one he had received from Natalie and dialed it.

He couldn't believe she had betrayed his trust like that. He couldn't believe he had actually trusted her.

After the fifth ring, the call went to voice mail. Sam barked his message loudly.

"Call me. Now."

He had barely hung up before the phone rang.

"It wasn't me," Natalie blurted out before Sam could say a word. "I swear to God."

"Screening your calls?" Sam asked.

"I needed to walk outside to get some privacy," Natalie said. "Sam, I swear. That wasn't me."

"Sure is one heckuva coincidence, don't you think?" Sam replied, unconvinced.

"I'm a junior reporter with absolutely no resources," she said. "You think I'm the only one that suspected there's more to this case than suicide? But I sat on it, like I promised. And now I got scooped."

"Who did it?"

"I don't know," she said. "The story hit several news sources at about the same time. Plus, social media. But none of the stories have any facts. They're just speculations. Apparently, you hadn't given them your little pep talk. And, by the way, none of them mention you."

Sam started to calm down. He didn't have any reason to believe Natalie, but he didn't have any reason to doubt her, either. But something about the whole thing seemed suspicious.

"Seems kind of weird that several news sources came up with the same rumor at the same time," he said.

"It's not that big of a town," Natalie said. "Rumors spread fast around here."

"I'm from a small town. I know how rumors can spread," Sam said. "But they tend to spread slowly. One person tells one person. This seemed to happen all at once."

"What are you getting at?" Natalie asked.

"You think you can do a little of that investigative

journalism you say you're good at and find out how this started?" Sam asked.

"How am I going to do that?" Natalie asked.

"I don't know. Ask around," Sam said. "That's reporter stuff."

"It's detective stuff," Natalie replied.

Sam chuckled.

"Like you said, sometimes our jobs are more alike than I want to admit," he said. "I'll be looking into it, too."

"What exactly are we looking for?" she asked.

"I feel like someone started this rumor on purpose," he said. "What I don't know is if it was to help me or to stop me."

44

***

"So, what are you going to do?" Carla asked.

She and Sam were waiting to be seated at Tessa's, courtesy of another restaurant reservation set up by the well-connected Ray.

"This way, please," the college-aged hostess said, grabbing two burgundy leather-bound menus.

"I don't think I have a choice," Sam finally answered Carla's question as they wove through the dimly lit restaurant. The walls, ceiling and floor were all covered in a dark, rich wood, which was highlighted by the gold leather upholstery on the chairs and stool backings. It looked both charming and luxurious at the same time.

They were led through the restaurant and out to a stunning dining patio. The rust-colored stone flooring glimmered under yellow lights strung between lush trees. Several white linen-covered round tables filled the patio, while a row of long tables were elegantly arranged under a chandelier in a lushly draped tented area. And it was all enclosed by a tall wooden fence covered in ivy. The effect was a Mediterranean oasis cut off from the rest of the word.

The hostess sat the couple down at a table nestled back in a corner and a server immediately appeared to take their drink orders.

"Are you just going to leave me hanging with that?" Carla asked. "You don't think you have a choice?"

"You know me, Carla," Sam said.

Carla smiled. "I do know you. And I know once you've sunk your teeth into something, you won't let go."

"I get what the chief is saying," Sam replied. "But I can't just let a killer walk free."

"If there even is a killer," Carla reminded him.

The waiter returned and sat a glass of Sauvignon Blanc in front of Carla and a tumbler of bourbon in front of Sam. He then began to recite the night's specials to the couple. Sam heard filet mignon and stopped listening. He knew Carla was going to go with the eggplant ravioli. Vanessa had made her promise to try it. But his ever-polite wife listened politely as the waiter explained in detail a seemingly endless list of special items. When he finished, they placed their orders and the waiter left.

"I always wonder if it's ruder to let them finish the whole thing, or to cut them off when you know what you want," Sam said.

"You think they have to memorize a whole new set of specials every night?" Carla asked. "For that reason alone, I could never be a server."

"Says the woman who knows every bone, muscle and nerve ending in the human body."

Carla laughed and the couple settled into a wonderful evening. An hour later, after they both had managed to resist the temptation of a tiramisu dessert, they were approached by an elegant woman wearing a long floral dress.

"Was your dinner to your liking?" the woman asked.

Her words were soft and distinguished, with a mild Italian accent.

"It was amazing," Sam said, leaning back in his chair.

The woman smiled, drawing even more attention to her high cheek bones and full lips.

"I'm very happy to hear that," she said. "You're from Texas, no?"

Sam grinned as he nodded. "My accent has given me away again."

"You wouldn't happen to be Sam Lawson, would you?" the woman asked.

Sam smiled, thinking he had once again been recognized from the serial killer documentary.

"I'm a friend of the Cannon family," she explained before turning to Carla. "And you must be Mrs. Lawson."

"Yes. I'm Carla."

She extended her hand, and the woman shook it gently.

"I'm Tessa Langly," she said. "This is my restaurant."

"It's incredible," Carla gushed. "The food. The atmosphere. Everything."

Tessa smiled again. "Thank you. You're so kind."

Then she turned her attention back to Sam.

"I heard about what happened to poor Frank," she said. "A suicide, they say?"

Sam could tell she was fishing for information, and he wasn't going to take the bait.

"That's what they're saying," was all he offered. "Despite what the press is trying to stir up."

"Did you know Mr. Cannon well?" Carla asked.

Tessa's smile grew a little broader and her cheeks flushed.

"We were very good friends," she said, sitting down at an open chair at the table.

"I know they hired you to look into it," she said

quietly. "I hope you're able to find the truth, which I can assure you was not suicide."

"You sound pretty certain of that," Sam replied.

"It's not like Frank," she said.

Sam leaned forward and spoke softly.

"If you know anything – anything at all – you can tell me."

She hesitated and looked around at the crowded restaurant.

"Come back tomorrow afternoon, when it's less crowded," she said.

As the waiter approached the table with the check, Tessa took it from him as she stood.

"Dinner is on me," she said. "Consider it both a welcome and a thank you gift."

Before Sam or Carla could pretend to protest, she was gone. Sam watched her as she walked past a patio entrance where a crowd was waiting to get in. In the back of the crowd, he spotted someone who looked familiar.

It was his mystery man.

Sam bolted up to get a better look, but a group of diners walked toward the exit, blocking his view. By the time, he could see again, the man was gone.

45

THE NEXT MORNING, Sam got up early to get a jump on a few other members of the Cannon clan. First up was William's wife. Julia. He still wasn't sure he was buying the story that she was just paying a trainer.

Having seen her car still in the driveway as he drove past William and Julia's house, Sam circled back, parking a block away. He hoped he wouldn't have to wait long. The neighborhood's early risers were staring at him suspiciously as they walked their dogs or took in a morning run. He had a feeling that this was the kind of neighborhood where residents were quick to call the cops about any strange car parked for no reason.

Luckily, it was no more than five minutes before Julia walked out her front door and got into her Escalade.

Thank goodness it's a car that's hard to miss, Sam thought as he hung back for a second before pulling on to the road behind her.

Assuming she was headed to the stables again, Sam was surprised when Julia made a right turn on VanDam Street. Sam wasn't completely oriented with the city, but he did know the track was in the other direction. He continued to follow her, past the Saratoga Hospital and out of town to a more rural area. The road had become a two-lane state highway that cut through wooded areas and pastures, occasionally broken up by small ranch-style houses or trailer homes. Finally, Julia turned right on a dirt road next to a block of multiple mailboxes. Sam drove past the mailboxes so he wouldn't arouse suspicion, but then pulled over to the shoulder, backing up until he could see down the dirt road. He squinted through the trees and was relieved to see Julia's SUV parked in front of a light blue mobile home.

Sam got out of his car and crept through the woods, staying crouched down to avoid detection. There were several mobile homes clustered along the dirt road. Julia had parked in front of the second one. That meant Sam had to get past the first one without being spotted by a nosy neighbor or barking dog.

He could see Julia wasn't in her car, so Sam could only assume she had already gone inside. The trailer park was quiet enough that he would have heard her knocking on the door. That meant that her host had been waiting for her, or she had just let herself in.

There were no cars in front of the first trailer, an old white double-wide. Sam hoped that meant that the occupants weren't home. He scurried quickly until he reached the structure, pressing against it so he couldn't be seen from any of the windows. Inside, the shrill voice of Sponge Bob was blaring from a TV. So much for someone not being home. Hopefully, they were too enthralled with their morning cartoon to notice the strange man lurking outside their window.

He pushed along the aluminum siding until he reached the back of the home. Once he turned the corner, he would be visible from where Julia was visiting. He peeked around the corner to look for another place to take cover. He saw one immediately. A large white propane tank.

Sam ran to the tank and crept to the edge, listening for any sign of life from inside. There was nothing. He peeked around the tank to make sure no one was watching him. All the curtains were pulled shut. Feeling more confident, Sam made his move, rushing to the rear of the home. He then slid along the length of the trailer, stopping to listen for any noise from inside. He was surprised to hear nothing. If anyone was talking inside, he would have heard every syllable. Feeling bold, he crept closer to the front door until he was so close he could have reached out and opened it.

That's when he heard the crunch of grass behind him. He spun around just in time to see a terra cotta flowerpot hit him in the head.

46

A SHARP, aching pain shot through his forehead as Sam pulled himself out of unconsciousness. As his eyes began to focus, he could see Julia leaning over him.

"Oh, thank God," she said.

Sam began to get his bearings. He was lying on the grass in front of the trailer home. The sun was bright and as he squinted, his headache only sharpened.

"What the hell?" he managed to grumble as he attempted to lift himself up on his elbows.

That's when he became aware of a man with short black hair and heavy five o'clock shadow standing next to Julia.

"I'm so sorry," the man said. "Are you okay?"

"Can you turn the sun down a bit," Sam said through squinted eyes.

The man and Julia helped him up and guided him inside the mobile home. They led Sam to a brown sofa and carefully set him down. The movement released another bolt of sharp pain through Sam's head. He reached up to touch the throbbing area above his right eyebrow, then looked at his bloody fingers.

"Let me clean it up," Julia said, attempting to dab it with a wet cloth.

Sam stiffened at the sting and grabbed the cloth out of her hand, applying pressure to the wounds.

"I thought you were coming after Julia," the man said.

Sam nodded. "I can see how it looked that way. No harm, no foul."

Julia introduced the man as Lance Rigalo, her horse's trainer.

"With everything that's been going on, I got spooked," Julia said. "I didn't know it was you."

"Are you going to be okay?" Lance asked. "It doesn't look like you'll need stitches."

"You have any ibuprofen or something?" Sam asked.

Julia jumped up and opened a kitchen cabinet, pulling out a bottle of Tylenol and shaking a couple into her hand.

"Don't be stingy with 'em," Sam said.

"She shook two more pills out of the bottle and

handed them to him, then grabbed a bottle of water from the fridge and handed that to him as well.

"Why were you following me?" Julia asked.

"Where are we?" Sam asked back.

"I live here," Lance said.

"I needed to discuss some issues with Lance," Julia said. "About my horse."

"Why not talk at the stables?" Sam asked.

"I wasn't going to the stables this morning," Lance said.

Sam looked at Lance. He was a good-looking man by anyone's standards. Dressed in a skintight white tank top undershirt and jeans, it was clear he was in great shape, too.

Sam smirked. "So how long have you two been having an affair?"

Lance and Julia glanced at each other, both unsure how to answer.

"I don't know..." Julia stammered.

"Come on," Sam interrupted. "You show up at his house in the early morning for a meeting? And Lance didn't even bother to get fully dressed? Plus, when I asked for Tylenol, you knew right where to find it."

"We work together," Lance said nervously. "Sometimes we map out strategy here."

"You're also barefoot," Sam said, pointing to Julia's feet.

Julia put one bare foot over the other, as if to hide them.

"This does not strike me as a 'take-your-shoes-off-when-you-enter' kind of house," Sam went on. "Besides, your boyfriend here is still wearing his."

"I put mine on when I saw you," Lance said, but Julia patted him on the shoulder to stop him.

"Did William put you up to this?" she asked.

"Relax. Nobody put me up to this," Sam said. "I just stumbled upon your little secret. And it can stay a secret as far as I'm concerned. I only care about who murdered your father-in-law. I'm also a little curious about who you were giving a pile of cash to yesterday."

"You have been following me!" Julia gasped.

"Not on purpose," Sam said. "Our paths just somehow keep crossing."

"She gave that money to me," Lance said. "At the stables, right? My training rate is low, but I get 'bonuses' in cash."

"So, you don't have to report them," Sam said.

"Yeah," Lance said with a shrug. "Everyone does it. It's no big deal."

The three studied each other, each assessing whether they could trust the other.

"I need to ask you some questions," Sam finally said to Julia. "About the night before Frank died. When you were all at their house. But while I'm here..."

Sam turned his attention to Lance.

"Where were you between one and four Wednesday morning?

47

LANCE WAS SHOCKED by the question.

"I, uh, I was here," he stammered. "Sleeping. I get up at 4 a.m.to get to the track by 5."

"Don't suppose anyone can corroborate that alibi," Sam said.

"I thought you said it was someone in the house," Julia said. "Lance wasn't there."

"But you were," Sam said, turning his attention to her.

"I was," Julia said indignantly. "And I already told the police that I was sound asleep during that time."

"Did you drink that night?" Sam asked.

Julia laughed. "When you have to babysit your drunk husband all night, you don't get the opportunity to enjoy more than a glass of wine."

"Did William get belligerent with anyone?" Sam asked. "Particularly his father?"

Julia shook her head. "Other than yelling a little bit, he was fine. And that was more William being animated than being a jerk. As far as Frank is concerned, William had nothing but respect for that man. Sometimes to a fault."

"When did you go to bed?" Sam asked.

"I remember Charlotte and Frank going to bed first," she said. "Then Charlotte came back down to set the security alarm."

"What time was that?"

"I don't know. Between ten and eleven? William and I went to bed shortly after that."

Sam noticed Lance clench his jaw whenever Julia mentioned her husband.

"You think anyone else knows about the two of you?" Sam asked, shifting gears.

Lance and Julia both shook their heads.

"There's no way," Lance said.

"We've gone to great lengths to keep this discreet," Julia added.

"Yeah. Even when it's a real pain in the ass," Lance remarked.

Julia shot him a scolding glance. Sam could tell they had had this conversation before.

"Not even Frank?" Sam asked. "I hear you had a tense conversation with him that night."

Julia gulped hard.

"I don't... no... I don't remember anything," she stammered.

"Come on, Julia. You're only making yourself look more guilty," Sam said. "He confronted you about this 'thing', didn't he?"

Julia looked at Lance, struggling for what to say.

"He knew?" Lance asked, clearly shocked. "Holy shit."

Julia let out a sigh of resignation.

"Yes. He knew," she said. "He told me that I needed to tell William, or he would."

"But then he conveniently killed himself later that night," Sam said.

"I didn't kill him!" Julia exclaimed. "And I was going to tell William. I really was."

"Was," Sam pointed out the word choice.

"Am," Julia corrected herself. "I am going to tell him. It's just... complicated."

"Oh, I bet it is," Sam said. "I imagine there is a lot of money at stake."

"You're out of your mind!" she exclaimed. "I would never kill Frank. Or anyone else, for that matter. Where do you get off accusing me? Me? Of all people! That whole family is filled with ungrateful, entitled monsters. And you're going to pick on me?"

Sam stood, wincing at the headache that hurt more when he moved.

"You're right," he said. "It's the concussion talking. I'll get out of your hair."

Julia grabbed his arm.

"Please. I need you to keep this to yourself for now. This isn't the time to add this drama to the mix."

Sam smiled.

"Don't worry. I'm not a homewrecker unless there's a reason for it," he said. "The way I see it, you're pretty much holding the peace in that family. You deserve to blow off a little steam."

He patted Lance on the shoulder as he walked past him.

"But I'm sure it's more than just that," Sam said with a smirk.

He walked out the door and grinned when he heard Lance's voice.

"Is that all this is to you?" Sam heard Lance saying to Julia.

Sam grinned, pleased with himself at the mess he'd created.

48

SAM LOOKED at the reflection of himself in the restaurant window. The ugly cut on his forehead was not a pretty sight, and it was made even worse by the embarrassing goose egg forming underneath it.

The front door to Tessa's was locked, so Sam knocked. A waiter emerged from the back and spoke through the door.

"Sorry, sir. We're not open yet," he said in a resigned voice obviously tired of saying this to people all morning. "Come back at 11:30."

"I'm here to see Tessa," Sam yelled back. "She's expecting me. Sam Lawson."

The waiter nodded and disappeared again. A few minutes later, Tessa emerged. Even though she was dressed more casually in slacks and a loose cotton blouse, she still radiated elegance. She unlocked the door for Sam.

"Good morning, Mr. Lawson," she said. "I didn't expect you so early."

Sam stepped inside a different Tessa's from the one he had seen the night before. Aside from it being quiet and mainly empty, the main dining area was brighter, partly because the empty booths allowed more of the gold upholstery to fill the room, but also because the overhead lights weren't dimmed.

Tessa immediately noticed Sam's injury and couldn't help but gasp.

"Oh my God, you're hurt," she said, turning to the waiter who had come to the door. "John, get the first aid kit and an icepack."

"I'm fine," Sam said. "The noggin's all made out of wood. No vital organs up here."

Tessa ignored him and led him through the kitchen to an office in the back. John met them there with a small first aid box. Tessa thanked him and nodded for him to leave. She forced Sam into a chair opposite her desk and opened the kit.

"What happened to you?"

"I had a fight with a house plant," Sam replied.

She looked into his eyes.

"Your pupils are dilated. You may have a concussion," she said as she swabbed a cotton ball with rubbing alcohol and dabbed it around the cut. Sam jolted back in pain.

"I'm fine. Really," he said. "It looks worse than it is."

But he let Tessa finish cleaning the wound and cover it with an adhesive bandage. It would allow her to feel more in control of the situation and less intimidated by him. Which meant she would hopefully be more open with him.

"So, was there something you wanted to tell me?" he asked. "Something you couldn't tell me last night?"

Tessa checked her medical work and once satisfied, carefully shut the first aid kit and walked behind her desk, sitting down.

"Not so much tell you, Mr. Lawson," she finally answered. "But show you."

She began to type a few things on to a computer keyboard, then spun her monitor around so they both could see it. The screen was separated into four quadrants, each displaying different black and white surveillance videos. Sam immediately recognized it as security camera footage. Tessa pointed at the quadrants one at a time.

"This is the dining area. This is the kitchen. This is the patio. And this one is the alley behind the restaurant."

She typed in a few more commands and the alley

footage filled the screen. Sam noted the date and time stamp.

It was Wednesday morning, 1:55 a.m. The morning Frank died.

Sam watched the footage. There was nothing much happening. Every once in a while, a car could be seen driving past the alley on an intersecting street. But that was it.

"What am I looking for?" Sam asked.

As if on cue, two men walked into view, their backs to the camera. The larger man was animated, he seemed upset. The other man was vehemently shaking his head.

"It looks like they're arguing," Sam said. "You know who they are?"

"That's Frank," she said, pointing to the large man.

Sam leaned in to get a better look.

"How can you tell?" he asked.

She froze the footage.

"That's his haircut," she said. "That's his build. That's his mannerisms. It's Frank."

Sam studied the image. You could make the argument that it was Frank. But it could honestly be anyone. Besides, how did Frank leave the house in the middle of the night without tripping off the home security system? It didn't add up.

"Do we ever see his face?" Sam asked.

Tessa sighed. "You sound like the police. Trust me. That's Frank Cannon."

Sam began to get the feeling that Tessa may know Frank better than she had previously said.

"What about the other guy?" Sam asked, giving her the benefit of the doubt.

Tessa allowed the footage to run a little longer. At one point, the other man turned to face Frank, revealing part of his face.

"Hold it! There!" Sam said.

Tessa froze the footage and Sam studied the image. The face was slightly blurred and half in the shadows, and the image itself was poor quality. But the face felt familiar to Sam.

Then it dawned on him.

"Holy shit," he muttered in shock.

49

EVEN THOUGH TESSA said she had shown the security footage to the police, he sent a screen capture from it to Detective Durant before calling him.

"Sam, I need to talk to you," Durant said.

"Did you just get the picture I sent you?" Sam asked, ignoring what Durant said.

Durant took a look as Sam explained that Tessa Langly believed it was Frank arguing with another man.

Durant started to argue that the man's face is never visible, but Sam cut him off.

"I know that's probably not Frank," he said. "I'm interested in the other guy."

He explained that it was the same man that had been following him ever since he started looking into the case.

"What do you mean 'following you'?" Durant asked.

"I keep seeing him everywhere I go," Sam said.

Durant laughed. "You've probably seen lots of the same people. It's not that big of a town."

"No. It's different," Sam argued. "I always catch him looking at me and then he disappears into the crowd. I know when I'm being tailed."

Durant sighed and zoomed in on the face.

"I can't make anything out of this," he said. "It's too pixelated. There are shadows. And it's blurry."

"It's all I've got to go on," Sam replied. "But we need to find him. I don't know how, but somehow, he's involved in all of this."

Detective Durant sighed.

"I'll do what I can. But you'd have better luck just walking around town until you see him again."

"That's exactly what I plan on doing."

"Sam, there's something else you need to know," Durant said. "That very well could be Frank."

50

SAM MET Carla for lunch and got her up to speed on the morning's activities, especially about Durant's discovery of the gap in the Cannon's home security system. She listened with interest and asked what his next steps were going to be.

"I need to rethink a lot of things," he said. "But I think that other guy may have some answers. I need to show the picture around town and see if anyone recognizes him. If I sent you the picture, could you show it around wherever you're going?"

"I'd be happy to," Carla said.

She examined the goose egg on his forehead.

"You're going to look great in the wedding photos," she said, only half joking.

"No one is going to be paying attention to me if you're in the same room," Sam replied.

Carla kissed him on the cheek. "You're sweet. But don't be talking that way around Vanessa. All eyes are supposed to be on the bride."

"But they won't be," Sam said in mock seriousness. "You're so beautiful you're going to steal the spotlight and your sister is going to get so upset and storm away from the alter. Then Ray is going to chase after her and trip and break his ankle. It's going to be all kinds of drama and absolutely no one will be paying any attention to a bandage on this ugly mug."

"Oh. That's how it's going to go, huh?" Carla said.

"I have no doubt in my mind," he said.

"I love how delusional you are," she said, this time kissing him on the lips. "Don't ever come to your senses."

"I don't think I'm even capable of that."

"You know," she purred with a mischievous smile. "I don't have to meet Vanessa again for a couple of hours."

She reached under the table and put her hand on Sam's thigh, leaning closer to him to speak softly in his hear.

"Can you think of a way we could kill a little time?"

An hour later, Sam lay naked in bed while Carla took a shower. His sizzled brain was short-circuiting back and forth between replaying what Durant had told him about the gap in the home security system and the mystery man in the video footage.

Knowing the home security system had been turned off for a few hours would explain how Frank was in the alley. But it also meant someone – anyone – could have come in the Cannon house to kill Frank later.

He tried to push the questions out of his head so he could relish his moment with Carla a little longer. But the case was seared into his bruised head and refused to go away. Finally, Sam gave up. He stood up and grabbed his jeans. Finding this mystery man was key, and he knew just where to start.

51

CHARLOTTE PEERED between the slats of the drawn blinds to look at the swarm of reporters and onlookers that were still gathered in front of her home. She had hoped that interest in her husband's death would quickly dissolve and be buried under the next wave of scandals and crises that seemed to roll in every day. But the crowd was getting larger. Local media was now joined by other reporters. From the looks of the news vans, they came from all over the country, specifically the areas where Cannon Autos had a presence.

She turned to face her family, most of whom were gathered in the living room at her request. Her desire to keep this story under control had become something of obsession. And the best way to control what everyone was saying was to keep them under her wing. A feat that had been much easier to accomplish before they had all become independent adults.

"Have you got hold of your brother yet?" she asked Peter.

"Still not answering," Peter replied, clearly tired of giving these updates. "Same with Donny."

"They're probably both at work," Julia chimed in. "William won't answer a call when he's with a customer."

"No. I called Trisha," Charlotte answered. "Neither one of them are there, and she doesn't know where they are."

Trisha was the regional sales manager who was also William's right hand at work.

"Probably on a killing spree," Peter said with a grin.

Rebecca threw an appropriately named throw pillow at him.

"Why do you always have to be an asshole?" she asked. "Did anyone try the clubhouse at the track?"

Julia shook her head.

"Not there either."

Charlotte paced the room.

"We can't just be prisoners in here forever, Mom," Rebecca said. "One of us should just go out and make a statement and be done with it. We've dealt with those jackals before."

"I'd like William to do that," Charlotte said. "Where is he?"

She was growing increasingly agitated and nervous.

"Why does William have to be the spokesperson?" Peter asked. "I'm better with those clowns than he is."

"You'll just dig us a deeper hole," Rebecca said.

"Screw you," Peter replied.

Rebecca ignored him, walking over to put an arm around her mother.

"Mom, why don't you come sit down? Take a breath."

Charlotte threw her daughter's arm off of her.

"I don't need to take a breath! I need my family to do what I ask them to do!"

Rebecca, Julia, and Peter were shocked by the uncharacteristic outburst.

"We're here, Mom," Peter said. "You can count on us."

They were all distracted by a noise at the back door as William and Donny walked in.

"Where the hell have you been?" Charlotte shouted.

The question/accusation caught both men by surprise. William looked to his sister for an explanation, but she could only shrug her shoulders.

"Sorry, Mom," William said, walking over and taking her in his arms. "We got here as quick as we could. We were up at the Corinth dealership."

"Cell service is awful up there," Donny chimed in. "We both got your messages when we got closer."

"Why didn't you call then, idiot?" Peter asked.

"We were almost here by then," William said.

Charlotte began to calm down. She told William about the media out front and how she needed him to go out and read a statement. William agreed readily.

"Do we have the statement yet?" he asked.

Charlotte nodded and pointed to a piece of paper on the mahogany credenza.

"You had it right there?" Peter asked. "I could have had this done already!"

William picked up the sheet of paper and read it.

"Alright. I'll read it. But we're all going out there," he said. "As a family. We don't want to give them anything to speculate about. But we're taking no questions. None. Got it?"

He walked over to the window and looked outside.

"This is getting out of hand," he said.

"It's that detective," Julia said. "He's stirring things up."

"He's just looking for the truth," Rebecca argued.

"We know the truth," Peter said. "Dad killed himself. End of story. I don't know why some of you refuse to accept that. There was no mysterious ninja. None of us did it. That Lawson guy is just taking our money."

"I told you I'll deal with him, and I will," William said. "Just haven't had a chance yet."

"Do you all think you can act as if you like each other for just a couple of minutes?

Charlotte asked.

"I've been doing it for years," Peter said.

"I'm not standing by him," Rebecca said.

"Come on," William said. "Focus on Dad. Think about what he'd want. Maybe even try to be a little sad about his death. Let's get this over with."

52

"What happened to you?" Arthur Gilford asked as he opened the door to his office.

"Rodeo injury," Sam deadpanned.

Gilbert started to probe further, but decided it was probably better if he didn't know. He motioned for Sam to follow him up the stairs.

Located in the heart of downtown, Gilford's office was on the second floor of a three-story red brick walk-up. The windows behind Gilford's desk looked down on the busy street.

"You've got a great people-watching perch up here," Sam said as he sat down in a chair facing Gilford's antique walnut desk. Gilford sat down behind the desk and swung his chair around to look out the large bay window.

"I have to be honest," he said. "It is an easy distraction. I have to pull the blinds most days so I can focus on work. But it's a great vantage point when they shut down the street for festivals and parades."

He turned back around to face Sam.

"But I doubt you're here to talk about my view," he said. "How's the car?"

"Car's great. Thanks again," Sam replied, pulling out his phone. "Are you aware of the security footage from behind Tessa's restaurant?"

Gilford shook his head, but Sam could tell a poker face when he saw one. He decided to play along and explained what was on the tape.

"You think it was Frank?" Gilford asked calmly.

"I don't know," Sam said.

"But what about the home security system?" Gilford asked.

"Yeah, there's some news about that, too."

Sam told a shocked Gilford about the home security system being turned off for a few hours in the middle of the night.

"But that could mean..."

"Yeah, it opens up all kinds of possibilities," Sam replied. "But I need two favors from you. The first is to keep all of this to yourself. The less people that know about the gap in the home security system, the better. I could also use your help with something else."

He turned his phone to a still-stunned Gilford to show him the screen capture of the mystery man from the security footage.

"I need to know who this is."

Gilford took the phone. Sam studied the lawyer's face carefully as he looked at the image.

"Do you have a better picture?" Gilford asked.

"Unfortunately, this is as good as it gets," Sam replied. "But I believe it's the same man I keep seeing all over town. The one I told you about."

Gilford looked harder, then shook his head.

"Sorry. I can't tell anything by this image," he said as he handed the phone back. "Why? Who do you think it is? What is this from?"

"The security footage behind Tessa's," Sam said. "It's the guy that was arguing with Frank. And it may be nothing. And he may not have even been talking to Frank. But I'm at the point where I'm grasping at straws. I'd appreciate it if you could share this picture with the family. See if any of them recognize him."

Gilford nodded cautiously.

"Wouldn't that be what I'm paying you to do?" he asked.

"I have a feeling they're not going to be honest with me," Sam said, fiddling with his phone. "I just sent you the picture. I appreciate it."

"So, no other progress?" Gilford asked.

Sam shook his head.

"But I feel like I'm close to a breakthrough," Sam said. "I think the guy in the picture could be it."

"I need to be candid with you, Mr. Lawson," Gilford said. "The family is growing frustrated with your investigation. In fact, they're putting pressure on me to terminate your services. I don't know how much longer I can hold them at bay."

Sam smiled.

"Is that why you leaked the rumor about Frank's death being a murder to the press?"

Gilford looked at Sam, playing dumb.

"I'm afraid I don't know what you're talking about," he replied.

Sam couldn't tell if he was lying or not.

"If it was to put more heat on me, it almost killed this whole investigation," Sam said.

"You think I leaked that rumor to the press?" Gilford asked.

"I think someone did," Sam said. "And you're about the only person I know who thinks Frank was killed."

"Sorry to disappoint you, Mr. Lawson. But I had nothing to do with it."

"Doesn't matter," Sam said. "I have a feeling if we figure out who that guy in the video is, we'll get a lot of the answers we need."

53

SAM SPENT the rest of the afternoon and evening visiting every bar, restaurant, and store in downtown Saratoga, seeing if anyone recognized the picture of the mystery man. He wasn't that surprised that no one did. Most looked at him suspiciously, wondering why he was even asking the question. Honoring his promise to stay discreet, Sam just told them that his friend was missing.

His search ended at the same restaurant where he had met Donny a couple of days earlier. Carla had plans with her sister, so Sam decided to sit at the outside bar. Since it was Friday, the inside bar was already packed. The outside bar wasn't as crowded. Sitting outside also afforded Sam the opportunity to watch the growing crowd of people walk down the street in front of him. Maybe he'd get lucky and spot his elusive John Doe.

He thanked the bartender for his Coke and moved to the wooden counter that faced the sidewalk. It was still nestled far enough back that he wouldn't be immediately visible to passers-by.

"Are you going to want something to eat?" a waitress asked him. "Full menu's not available at the bar, but all the good stuff is."

She handed him a menu and told him she'd be back in a bit. Sam turned to take in the scene that was growing more and more festive as the sun set. Young people were packing into open-air bars up and down Putnam Street, each making its own contribution to the mash-up of music, laughter, and intoxicated whoops that filled the air. Scattered between the festivities of the bars, people dined inside cozy restaurants, oblivious to the fact that they were on full display through the large restaurant windows, like some sort of bizarre zoo exhibit.

Sam chuckled to himself. Ten years ago, he could have caused some serious trouble in this town. Still, that wild man was always in the shadows. Just waiting for permission to come out and play.

Four hours later, the wild man was close to being pulled off the bench. Sam still occupied the same spot, having eaten one of the best burgers he had ever tasted.

He had also been befriended by a group of middle-aged men from Long Island. The Long Islanders playfully poked fun at Sam's "funny accent." Sam was quick to point out that in his parts, they would be the ones talking funny, and after an hour of shared drinks, they were all trading pronunciations of words.

"What's this? What's this?" one of the men asked, holding up a glass of water.

"Wuh-ter," Sam replied, amplifying his twang for effect. "What do y'all call it?"

"Waw-duh," the man replied back.

They all laughed.

"I can't even make my mouth make that sound," Sam said.

The Long Islanders kept repeating "waw-duh" as Sam tried to mimic them.

"Wait. What was that other word you said?" another Long Islander asked. "You all?"

"You all?" Sam asked with mock offense. "I ain't got time for that. It's 'y'all'. One syllable. What do y'all say?"

The men all looked at each other, not sure what an equivalent would be. Finally, one of them spoke up.

"Awl-uh-yooz," he said.

The other Long Islanders laughed in recognition and then laughed even harder when Sam tried to imitate them. He stood up and took a tough mobster-like stand.

"Hey! Awl uh yooz. How's about some wawduh? I need it for my dawg."

"Get outta here," the largest Long Islander said before standing up and bowing his legs like a cowboy. Then he somehow managed to combine a Texas and Long Island accent together.

"Howdy, y'awll. I reckon' I better mosey out to the ranch."

"What the hell was that, Bob?" one of the other Long Islanders asked.

The waitress brought over a tray filled with whiskey shots. So far, Sam had been able to say no, but he was having such a good time, the moment had finally got the best of him. To the Long Islanders' delight, he grabbed one of the shot glasses and raised it in the air. They all cheered, and Sam slammed it back. Sam welcomed the taste like an old friend and immediately requested another round from the bemused waitress.

If you're going to visit Saratoga, you might as well enjoy the full experience, he rationalized.

The second round of shots came fast and Sam threw his back immediately. Just as he was about to order yet another round, he happened to look out at the passing crowds.

And there he was.

The mystery man was on the other side of the street and was looking down.

He hasn't noticed me yet, Sam thought, as his heart started racing.

Without taking his eyes off the man, Sam pulled out a wad of bills from his pocket and threw it on the table.

"Guys. It's been fun, but I gotta go."

The men started protesting, but Sam wasn't paying attention. He was quickly walking out of the bar, his head down to avoid being seen. He crossed the street and began to slowly get closer to the man who was casually walking down the street, unaware he was being followed. When the man suddenly stopped, Sam ducked into a restaurant doorway. Unable to see the man from his hidden spot, Sam peered around the corner to see if the man had continued walking.

But he was still standing in the same spot, looking directly at Sam. The second he recognized who was looking back at him, the man turned and ran, quickly disappearing into a mass of bodies emerging from a club.

"Not this time," Sam muttered, as he took off after him, fighting through the crowd.

54

SAM PUSHED through the crowd to see the man charging up Caroline Street. Clusters of people were either filing into or spilling out of the bars on either side of the road. Those crowds, coupled with the steep incline of the road, made it hard for Sam to catch up with the fleeing man. As he struggled up the street, he kept his eye on his target, watching him top the hill and turn left.

A few seconds later, an out-of-breath Sam reached the top of the street and made the same left. But the man was gone. Sam walked down the street, looking for any possible avenue of escape. This street had more closed retail shops than open restaurants and bars, so there were fewer places where the man could have gone.

Sam looked in each open door. He figured if a man

ran through a restaurant, it would catch the attention of the other patrons, who would probably all be looking in the man's direction.

Everything seemed normal in the first two restaurants, but when he reached the large Mexican restaurant a few doors further down, the patrons were definitely all looking toward the back of the dining area.

Sam ran inside, following the object of everyone's attention. He pushed through the crowded bar into the kitchen. Pots and pans were still rattling on the floor from something so Sam knew he was on the right path.

"Police!" Sam shouted. "Where'd he go?"

A busboy pointed to a backdoor and Sam took off with renewed energy. He rushed out into the alley just in time to see someone running into the backdoor of another restaurant.

Sam ran through the doors and crashed into a rack of pans that had been pushed in the way. The clanging sound of crashing pans was deafening as Sam toppled over them. Yelling out apologies, he scrambled to his feet and kept going. Into the dining area, where the diners had rushed out of the way while a madman barreled through the restaurant, knocking over chairs and tables along the way.

Sam followed the same path of chaos, which led him out the front of the restaurant. He was back on Caroline Street. He looked down the hill and spotted his man among the sea of partiers. As he ran after him, he saw him duck into a bar at the end of the street.

By the time Sam got to the bar, he was relieved to see the club's bouncers had done his work for him. They had grabbed the man as he tried to race into their bar and were holding him in a choke hold as he flailed around on the ground.

Sam walked up to them, so out of breath he could barely breathe.

"Thanks, boys," Sam said, flashing his detective's badge quickly.

He pulled out a pair of handcuffs he still carried. If nothing else, they helped him look official. As the bouncers held the man steady, Sam slapped on the cuffs.

"I can take it from here," he said.

"You sure?" one of the bouncers said. "You don't look too good."

Sam waved him off, still gasping for air which made it hard to talk.

"Wanted. In seven states," Sam finally replied in short bursts. "I'll have some... uniforms stop by... for your names. Pretty good reward."

The bouncers were so excited about the prospect of a reward they didn't ask for a closer look at Sam's badge. Once handcuffed, the man succumbed to his fate and stopped fighting, much to Sam's relief. Sam pulled the man out of the bar and into the street, where a crowd of onlookers had gathered. Many had their phones taking video. Sam kept his head turned away as much as possible as he led his captor around the corner toward the police station.

As soon as they got past the crowded street, things quickly quieted down.

"I've been looking all over for you," Sam said, slowly regaining his breath. "We need to talk."

55

"I KNOW YOU'RE NOT A COP," the man said as Sam led him down the street.

"And I know you don't want to get the cops involved," Sam replied. "Otherwise, you would have said something back there."

Sam looked behind him. A few onlookers were still watching them. A few were filming with their phones. As they turned the corner by the police station, Sam prayed they wouldn't follow. He quickly pushed the man into a dark alley and led him behind some trash bins so they couldn't be seen.

"Why were you running from me?" Sam demanded as he pushed the man face first against the brick wall.

"You were chasing me," the man exclaimed.

"Let's not chicken and egg this, asshole," Sam said.

"You've been keeping an eye on me for a few days now and I want to know why."

"Can you at least take these cuffs off?" the man asked.

Sam spun him around, so they were facing each other.

"I lost the key," Sam said. "Who are you?"

"Jimmy."

"I didn't ask for your name, numb nuts," Sam replied. "I want to know who you are."

"Just a guy," Jimmy said.

"You gotta stop lying to me, Jimmy," Sam said. "You can tell me the truth, or I can take you across the street and you can tell the police. They're looking for you, too."

"I didn't do anything!"

"How do you know Frank Cannon?" Sam asked.

"Who? I don't know who that is."

"Why were you arguing with him the other night?"

"I don't know what you're talking about."

"This dumb act is getting old, Jimmy. There's security footage of you arguing with Frank Cannon in an alley a couple of nights ago."

Jimmy studied Sam's face. Sam couldn't tell if he had no idea what Sam was talking about or if he was buying time to come up with another lie.

"I remember some guy yelling at me. I was drunk

and I got sick on the sidewalk. Then this guy comes out of nowhere and starts laying into me," Jimmy said. "I didn't want any trouble, so I walked away, but he followed me and started yelling."

"What was he yelling?"

"I don't know," Jimmy said. "It didn't make sense. He'd be yelling about how people like me are ruining the town and then stuff about everyone wants his money. Most of it was just him cussing at me."

"And then he just walked away?"

"Yeah. Like he just ran out of steam."

"Which direction did he walk?"

"To the end of the alley, I guess," Jimmy said. "I turned and got the hell out of there before he came back."

Sam didn't believe a word of it, but he knew he wasn't going to get the truth.

"So why were you really following me?" Sam asked. "Why do you keep showing up everywhere I go?"

"I could ask you the same question," Jimmy said.

"Why are you lying to me, Jimmy?" Sam asked.

"Why would I lie?"

"I don't know," Sam said as he pulled out his phone. "But I'm going to find out."

He dialed a number into his phone and waited for an answer.

"Detective Durant. I've got a present for you."

56

SAM AND DETECTIVE DURANT looked through the one-way mirror into the interrogation room where Jimmy was patiently drumming his fingers on the table.

"I can't keep him," Durant said.

"He's the key to all of this," Sam said. "I'm sure of it."

A uniformed cop brought a manila folder into the room and handed it to Durant.

"We got a hit," the cop said.

Durant studied the folder.

"He's had a few priors," Durant said. "Petty stuff. Shoplifting. Bad checks. But he did do a year for 'breach of computer security'."

"He's a hacker?" Sam asked.

"Apparently a pretty good one," Durant replied.

"Released after a year as part of an agreement to consult the feds on ID theft stuff."

"Give me that," Sam said, grabbing the folder from Durant and storming into the interrogation room.

Before Durant could stop him, Sam sat down in front of Jimmy.

"So, you're a computer whiz, huh?" he asked.

"You going to arrest me for that?" Jimmy asked with a smirk.

"Did you steal Frank Cannon's identity?" Sam asked. "Blackmail him to get it back?"

"Do you even know how ID theft works?" Jimmy asked.

Sam opened the folder and read it out loud.

"James Goodwin. From Pittsburgh, PA."

Jimmy sighed.

"Look, if you're not going to charge me with anything, then I'm gonna go."

"I know you are somehow involved in Frank Cannon's death," Sam said. "And I will prove it."

Jimmy shook his head. "You don't know shit."

"Then enlighten me," Sam replied.

Jimmy leaned forward.

"I didn't kill Frank Cannon," he said. "But he's not the saint you think he is."

"So, you do know who he is," Sam said.

Jimmy stared into Sam's eyes like he wanted to tell him something, but then he leaned back.

"Either let me go or get me a lawyer," he said. "I'm done talking."

57

CARLA WAS READING a book in bed when Sam returned to their hotel room. She could tell right away that he was upset.

"Oh no," she said. "What happened?"

Sam threw his key card, phone, and wallet on the dresser, and told her about his adventure with Jimmy and how Durant had let him go.

"And then! Then, he ripped me a new one for detaining him with handcuffs."

"Well, he does have a point there," Carla said. "I mean, the guy could have pressed charges against you."

"But he wouldn't have," Sam said. "Because he's hiding something."

"So, what are you going to do now?" Carla asked.

"At least I got a better picture of the guy. And we found out a little bit about him."

"Well, at least that's a start," Carla said.

"It won't even matter if this guy takes off, which he most likely will now," Sam said.

"I don't know," Carla argued. "Something brought him here. And he's stuck around after Frank died. There's got to be some reason. And you have a better picture now. Maybe you can show that to the Cannons and see what they know."

Carla's voice of reason was starting to calm Sam down.

"Maybe. Although I'm beginning to think nobody in that family is capable of telling the truth about anything."

"Speaking of which," Carla said, grabbing a slip of paper from the nightstand. "There was a note for you at the front desk."

She handed the slip of paper to Sam.

"Seems Peter Cannon wants to meet with you."

58

SAM ARRIVED at the diner at 8 a.m., as directed by Peter's note. It was a small, unassuming diner off the beaten path. A tiny space consisting of six booths along the front window and an eight-person counter on the other side of the narrow aisle. In the back, there was a small space for a table and another booth. It was also packed.

Sam spotted Peter sitting in the back corner booth, facing away from the other patrons and wearing a black hoodie pulled down over his head. Sam sat down opposite the youngest Cannon.

"This place must be good to be this packed," he said. "Kind of an out of the way spot."

"Trust me. It's the best," Peter said.

"I obviously got your note," Sam said, done with the small talk. "What's up?"

Before Peter could answer, they were interrupted by the waitress. She looked to be in her mid-thirties. Her spiked, jet black hair and tattoos that ran up and down her arms would have made her pretty intimidating, but her friendly smile immediately put Sam at ease.

"Give me the Nutella French Toast and a side of bacon," Peter said, then turning to Sam. "Dude, you gotta get the French Toast."

Sam looked at the laminated single page menu.

"I'm not much of a French toast guy," he said.

"You like corned beef hash?" the waitress asked. "We make the best."

Sam grinned. "Now you're talking. Two eggs over easy. Corned beef hash. Wheat toast. And black coffee."

"You ever had chorizo hash?" the waitress asked. "It's pretty good."

"Oh, yeah. Get him that," Peter said. "I promise you. You'll thank us both."

Sam nodded. "Chorizo it is."

The waitress wrote it all down and walked away.

"So, your mother let you out of house arrest?" Sam asked.

Peter laughed uncomfortably. "I ventured out at my own risk."

"You snuck out, didn't you" Sam asked with a smile. "Rebecca showed me the secret getaway on the back fence."

Peter laughed.

"Guilty. They're just all afraid I'm going to say something stupid to the press. But I'm careful."

"I can see," Sam replied, pointing to Peter's hoodie.

The waitress returned to serve them both coffee.

"Cream and sugar's on the table," she said as she walked away.

As soon as she walked away, Sam continued.

"So, why'd you want to meet?"

"I know you already talked to Rebecca and William."

"And Julia. And Donny. And Gilford. Even your mom."

"So why not me?"

"I just hadn't got to you yet."

Peter fidgeted in his seat.

"I know those guys all probably talk shit about me."

"No more than anyone else," Sam replied.

"Like what?" Peter asked. "What'd they say?"

"About you?"

"Yeah," Peter replied.

"They said your dad was going to cut you off," Sam said.

No one had done more than just suppose it, but Sam wanted to see how Peter reacted.

Peter shook his head, pissed.

"That's total bullshit."

"I'm hearing all sorts of things from all sorts of people."

"I bet William told you that," Peter replied. "Did he also tell you that Dad wasn't going to promote him?"

Sam tried to hide his surprise.

"Did your dad tell you that?"

Peter laughed. "Didn't have to. I heard it myself. That very night. That's why I wanted to meet you."

"What did you hear, Peter?"

"We had dinner and were just hanging out around the table. William was drunk, as usual. And Dad got up and went to the library. About five minutes later, William followed him. I knew something was up. So, I excused myself to go to the bathroom."

"But you really went to listen at the door," Sam said.

"No, idiot," Peter said. "Everyone would have seen me. I really did go to the bathroom... downstairs."

"The basement?"

"It's a fully-finished basement, Cowboy," Peter said. "My old room, a game room, and a bathroom. It's an old house. The vents are all connected. And the basement bathroom is directly below the library."

"So? What did you hear?"

"Well, I couldn't make out a lot of it. Only when they raised their voices."

"So did you hear anything or not?" Sam asked, growing impatient.

"I heard Dad yelling at him about how much he drinks and what an embarrassment he is. And I heard William yelling back to Dad to mind his own business. But then I heard Dad yell 'That's why I'll never turn the business over to you.'"

"Did William respond?"

Peter laughed.

"Oh, did he. Most of it was just his normal drunk-ass name-calling. But then he said, 'You're going to wish you never said that, old man.'"

He stopped to have another sip of coffee.

"And then what?" Sam asked.

"What do you mean 'then what?'?" Peter scoffed. "He threatened him. Right then and there. And then the jackass winds up dead a few hours later? And then, guess who immediately makes their move to run the company? Sounds pretty straight forward to me."

Sam thought about everything Peter had told him.

"Would you be willing to testify to that?" he asked.

"Hell, no," Peter said. "I'm telling you this in confidence. If my mom ever found out I ratted on my own brother, she'd definitely kick me out of the family."

"Well, this information is kind of worthless then," Sam said.

"No, it's not," Peter said. "It tells you where you should be focusing your attention. It's William. He's the killer."

Sam thought about what Peter had said.

"And I know what you're thinking," he continued. "I must be a real dick to turn my brother in like that. But he's a dick. If he's going to throw me under the bus, I'm yanking him down with me."

59

SAM LEFT the diner and immediately called Gilford, telling him he needed to talk. Since it was Saturday, Gilford wasn't in the office, so he asked Sam to meet him at his home. Fifteen minutes later, Sam was ringing Gilford's doorbell.

Gilford opened the door wearing a green polo shirt and tan khakis. It was as casual as Sam had ever seen the man.

"You'll have to excuse me," Gilford said. "I wasn't expecting guests. Would you like some coffee?"

Sam declined, as he was starting to buzz from all the coffee he had at the diner. "I will have a glass of water, if you don't mind."

The two men went into the large, stark white

kitchen. Other than the area around the stainless-steel espresso machine, the entire kitchen was spotless, and the counters were gleaming. Sam got the feeling that Gilford didn't do much cooking.

Gilford pulled a water bottle from the built-in refrigerator and grabbed the cup of espresso that was already prepared.

"Shall we go out to the patio?" he asked.

Sam was growing a bit restless, so he started telling Gilford about Peter's accusations. But without mentioning Peter, as promised, it quickly became a watered-down rumor.

Gilford sat down at the round patio table and motioned for Sam to sit opposite him.

"So, you're saying you heard that Frank had told William he wasn't going to turn the business over to him? And that William threatened him?" Gilford asked. "Where did this happen? Who heard it?"

"That, I'm not sure about," Sam lied.

Gilford laughed.

"Well, that's a very unoriginal rumor. Those two had that argument at least once a week, and it always ended the same way: With William storming off then calming down once he realized, deep down, that his father was right. William is a decent businessman, but Frank was a savvy one. There's a big difference. And William knows it."

"But maybe William finally had enough," Sam suggested.

"Maybe," Gilford said. "But not likely. To be honest, without the face of Frank, I don't know how long the company is going to last. William knows that, too. He's panicked. We all are."

Sam wasn't convinced but knew he wouldn't be getting anywhere else with Gilford on the subject. He decided to switch gears.

"Also, I caught up with my stalker last night."

Gilford sat up in his chair.

"You did?"

Sam pulled out his phone and showed the image of Jimmy Goodwin to the lawyer, explaining who he was and where he was from. Even though Gilford maintained a practiced, even expression, Sam caught a glint of panic in his eyes.

"He claims he doesn't know anything about Frank or the family. He look familiar to you?"

Gilford shook his head and leaned back.

"I'm afraid he doesn't," he said. "I've never seen him."

"Peter said the same thing," Sam said.

He noted Gilford's surprise at the name.

"Oh. I met Peter for breakfast," Sam said. "This great place. They make the most amazing chorizo hash."

"What did Peter have to say?" Gilford asked.

"You know Peter," Sam said. "He's all gas, no engine."

"So is your mystery man another dead end?" Gilford asked.

Sam shook his head.

"I don't know. For one, I don't buy his story at all. I think he's lying about what went on in the alley. And it got me thinking. What if he was blackmailing Frank?"

"About what?"

"I don't know. Some hidden secret or family scandal," Sam replied. "Something Frank had buried and didn't want uncovered. Whatever it is, maybe Frank refused to pay."

"Wouldn't this Jimmy person just release the information?" Gilford asked.

"Unless he was bluffing," Sam said. "He's pissed at Frank and decides to take his revenge."

Gilford finished his espresso.

"It doesn't make sense. For one thing, there are no secrets. All the family scandals, and there have been plenty, have already been aired publicly, much to Frank's disappointment. It was something he was always trying to overcome. And he ran a clean business. He prided himself on that."

"But what if..."

"I need you to focus on what is, and not on what if,"

Gilford said, clearly agitated. "I've already told you the family is growing tired of you and, frankly, I'm beginning to feel the same way."

60

EVEN WITH GILFORD'S very sound argument against blackmail, Sam still wasn't convinced that Jimmy didn't have a connection to Frank's murder. And that it was because Frank was hiding something. Knowing that the home office had been scrubbed down, Sam decided Frank's dealership office was a good place to do some digging.

It was nearing noon on a Saturday morning, and the dealership was bustling with customers.

Perfect, Sam thought. *They'll keep everyone distracted.*

He was able to easily walk past the receptionist desk to the back offices. There were no construction workers to deal with this time, and even though the lights were on in all the offices, no one was in any of them. Before Sam slipped into Frank's office, he snuck far enough down the hall to see if William was working. As he got close, he could hear William at his desk.

Sam would need to keep him occupied for a while. Fortunately, he had prepared for that. He texted Carla a quick message.

PLEASE CALL HIM.

Within fifteen seconds, William's office phone was ringing.

"Hello?" William answered. "Yes. This is William Cannon. How can I help you?"

Knowing Carla would ask enough questions to keep William busy for as long as Sam needed, he returned to Frank's office.

Not surprisingly, the laptop was gone. William probably picked that up immediately upon Sam's last visit. But other than that, the office seemed untouched. The dust had been cleaned up, but all the files seemed to be in the same place.

Sam sat down behind the desk again, surveying the office for any obvious clue he might have missed. He opened the middle desk drawer. Nothing but a few pens, pencils, and paper clips. The side drawers were both locked, so Sam nabbed one of the paper clips and twisted it up to form a lock pick. He inserted it in the top lock and moved it around until he felt the catch. Then with a few jiggles, the drawer opened.

Again, there wasn't much of consequence. Although

Sam wasn't even really sure what he was looking for. But there were no secret journals or ransom letters. Just a few more office supplies, some blank yellow notepads and a few fluorescent Post-it Notepads. Sam was about to shut the drawer when something caught his eye.

A tiny red splotch on the top of one of the fluorescent yellow Post-it Notepads. It was so small, that Sam probably wouldn't have noticed it if it hadn't been contrasted against the bright yellow background. Maybe it was from a red pen. Or maybe it was blood.

He would have to leave that up to the police department's forensic team, but Sam was desperate enough to make the assumption it was blood. But why stop there? Why not assume, because it was blood, that it was blood from Frank's death? That would mean the notepad had been removed from the house after Frank's murder and then thrown in the office drawer.

On the other hand, the blood could have been from a paper cut. Or it was just red pen ink. As he thought about it, he realized it didn't matter. The police weren't going to look at any more evidence. But that didn't mean it still couldn't help the case. He picked the notepad up by the edges and sat it on the desk. All the Post-it Notes were blank, so Sam would try to see what was written on the last Post-it Note removed.

He grabbed a pencil from the middle drawer and, carefully avoiding the red dot, lightly shaded the entire

Post-it Note. If Frank had written on the Post-it Note above it, it might have left an indentation on this note. Sure enough, letters seemed to emerge from the shading. While every letter wasn't completely legible, Sam was able to make out what was written:

GOLD PADDOCK CONSULTING

He texted Carla again.

YOU CAN LET HIM GO NOW. THANKS.

Then Sam grabbed the Post-it Notepad and headed for William's office.

61

WILLIAM WAS HANGING up the phone just as Sam arrived at his office. The sight of the detective immediately deflated him.

"What the hell are you doing here?" he demanded. "And how did you even get back here?"

Sam ignored him and walked up to the desk.

"What is Gold Paddock Consulting?" he asked.

"How the hell would I know?" William asked.

"You don't do business with them?" Sam pushed.

"I don't know," William replied. "We do business with lots of companies."

"But you've never heard of Gold Paddock Consulting?"

"I told you. No. Here. You want me to look them up?" he swiveled his computer monitor around so Sam could see. "They have an amazing tool you can use. Called Google."

William typed in the name, but nothing came up.

"Doesn't exist."

"Doesn't show up in a Google search," Sam said. "More common than you think. Do you have a list of vendors or contractors?"

William sighed, realizing he was going to have to placate Sam on this.

He opened up a program on his computer and began to search.

"You mind telling me what this is for?" he asked. "Might save us a lot of time."

"Do you have the name there?" Sam asked, ignoring William.

"No. No Gold Paddock Consulting," William said. "Are you satisfied yet?"

"Where's your dad's laptop?" Sam asked.

"Okay. We're done here," William said. "Has Gilford talked to you yet? We're done with you."

"I can have the police get a warrant," Sam bluffed. "But I'm trying to be discreet here."

William groaned.

"I'm not doing anything until you tell me what this is about," William said.

Sam showed him the notepad.

"I think this notepad came from your father's home

office," Sam said. "And it looks like that's what he had written down."

William reached for the notepad, but Sam snatched it back.

"Sorry. This could be evidence. The less people touching it, the better. Now, what about your dad's laptop?"

"So, you found something in his office here and you think it came from his home office," William said. "And you think you can get a warrant because of that?"

"Not because of that," Sam said, showing the splotch of red. "Because of this."

"What is that?" William asked.

"We can get a warrant and find out," Sam said. "Or you can get your dad's laptop."

William opened a desk drawer and pulled out the laptop.

"Check to see the last files he had opened," Sam said.

William opened the laptop. He dragged the cursor over a few tabs to display a list of Recent Items.

"Last thing he had opened was the bookkeeping program," William said as he opened the file.

A spreadsheet full of numbers filled the computer screen.

"It's open to his expenditures," William said. "Mainly travel expenses and stuff."

He scrolled through the list and stopped at one item.

"Holy shit," he said. "There it is."

Sam squinted at the screen until he found the entry.

"According to this, we paid Gold Paddock Consulting $10,000 a few weeks ago."

"Can you check to see if that's the only time you paid them?" Sam asked.

William nodded and entered a new command. A spreadsheet popped up on the screen.

"What the hell?" William said.

"If I'm reading this right," Sam said. "It's showing that $10,000 was paid to them about every month for the past..."

"Fourteen months," William said, finishing the thought.

He instantly picked up his phone and dialed a number.

"Donny, are you in the office? That's okay. I'm here with Mr. Lawson. I'm going to put you on speaker."

"What's going on?" Donny asked.

"What do you know about Gold Paddock Consulting?" William asked.

Donny repeated the name several times, letting it roll around in his memory.

"Let me check," he finally said.

Sam could hear Donny hitting the keypads on his own laptop.

"Why are you asking?" he asked as he typed. "What's going on?"

"Just checking on a few things," Sam said, motioning to William to not offer anything more.

"Here it is," Donny said. "Oh, yeah. I knew it sounded familiar. This was one of your dad's things. I think they were a location strategy firm your dad used a lot."

"Used for what?" William asked.

"Coming up with new locations or something?" Donny seemed to be guessing. "I remember seeing it the first time about a year ago or something. I asked your dad about it and that's what he told me."

"Do you have an address?" Sam asked. "A name? What about cancelled checks? Do you know where they went?"

"Frank always wrote out a check and hand-delivered it," Donny said. "But that would mean there would be records of the check clearing the bank. I'd have to call the bank for a copy, though. They won't be able to respond until Monday."

"First thing, Donny," William said. "Got it?"

"Sure thing," Donny said. "You still haven't told me what this is all about."

"I'll fill you in later," William answered before hanging up.

He turned to Sam with a relieved smile.

"Well, there you go," he said. "A location consulting company."

Sam smiled and stood, but not before noticing the sweat on William's forehead.

62

WILLIAM PROMISED Sam he would let him know what he found out, but he needed to get some work done before he had to leave for an appointment — something Sam already knew about. He had seen the note on William's desk calendar.

GRACE FUNERAL HOME 3:00

Sam drove to the funeral home just outside of town and parked down the street, far enough away to not be noticed, but close enough to see what was going on. He figured William wouldn't be going to a funeral home by himself, so more than likely, the entire family was meeting there.

Gilford must have come earlier, as he stepped out the front door of the funeral home to greet Rebecca and

Peter, who arrived together. William arrived soon after. Sam looked around for Charlotte but couldn't see her. Then he saw Donny pull up.

That's odd, Sam thought. *This is true family affair. Why would Donny be here?*

After everyone went inside, Sam got out of his car and walked up to the funeral home. He peeked inside the door, and seeing no one in the main lobby, ducked into a hallway to the immediate right. Following the muffled bickering of the Cannons, he slipped into an empty storage room. A sliver of light from under another door cut through the darkness. Sam navigated through rows of storage boxes to get to it, then quietly turned the door handle cracking the door open just enough for Sam to peer into the arrangement room where the Cannons had gathered around a table. Fortunately, several floral arrangements were on display directly in front of the door, camouflaging Sam's vantage point. It made it hard for him to see everything, but he had no problem hearing.

"Why is he here?" Rebecca asked William, nodding at Donny. "This is a family meeting. Real family."

"I needed to talk to him," William said.

He motioned for Donny to join him at the corner of the room, where the two began to talk in hushed tones.

"This is ridiculous," Rebecca said. "He's turning this into a business meeting."

"Why do you act surprised when he keeps doing the same thing over and over?" Peter laughed.

"If I could get everyone's attention," the funeral director said softly.

He was a short, stocky man with a quiet demeanor and dark suit.

Sam couldn't be sure, but it looked like William and Donny were having an argument. He couldn't help but assume it was about Gold Paddock Consulting.

"Guys!" Rebecca said loudly. "Not the time or place."

The two men sat down, and William whispered to Rebecca.

"What?" she said after hearing what William had to say. "That's ridiculous."

"What's ridiculous?" Peter asked. "What's going on?"

"Excuse me," the funeral director spoke a little more loudly. "If I could get your attention."

But no one was even aware of him anymore.

Rebecca shook her head.

"It doesn't make sense," she said to William and Donny, not even trying to be quiet about it. "A location service? Daddy didn't believe in them. He didn't trust anyone else to do that. I even offered to do it, but he said that he liked doing it."

"Yeah, but Becca, let's be honest," William said, relieved not to have to whisper any longer. "He pretty much didn't want you involved in anything."

"Barefoot and in the kitchen, baby," Peter laughed.

"I just need a few minutes of your time," the funeral director said.

"Screw you," Rebecca snapped at Peter.

"I'm sorry?" the funeral director asked, stunned.

"No, not you," Rebecca said. "This idiot."

"Oh, I'm the idiot," Peter said. "Really?"

"Maybe he got too busy," Donny said. "They started right when we added locations in three new states. And since it's always the same amount, I'm assuming it was a retainer fee."

"Do you need the room for a few minutes?" the funeral director asked, clearly growing agitated. Again, he was ignored.

"Yeah, well those payments need to stop right now," William said.

"Way ahead of you," Donny replied. "The payments would have to go through me now, anyway. Now that your dad is gone."

The funeral director shut his planner.

"I'll be in my office," he said. "Let me know when you're ready for me."

As he walked out of the room, Sam's phone lit up with an incoming text. He was so relieved he had put everything on silent. The last thing he needed was to be discovered lurking in a funeral home storage room.

The text was from Charlotte:

I NEED TO TALK TO YOU ASAP. THERE'S SOMETHING YOU NEED TO KNOW.

63

SAM WALKED through Congress Park again. This time, he headed toward the large, red brick building just beyond the stream. He looked at the three-story red brick building.

Sure doesn't look like any casino I've seen before, Sam thought.

When he had walked past it on his first trek through the park, he had assumed it was just another historic building that had been converted into offices. As he walked up the steps of the main entrance, he still had no reason to feel differently.

Where were the crowds? The familiar sound of casino bells and buzzers?

Maybe it's just really well soundproofed, he thought.

When he walked inside, he became even more

confused. It looked like some sort of historic banquet hall, but definitely not a casino. He stepped into the large empty hallway, looking for any sign of life. It was so quiet, Charlotte's voice startled him.

"Hello, Mr. Lawson," she said, her voice echoing in the empty space. "Thank you for meeting with me."

Sam turned to see Charlotte standing in the entrance of what looked to be some sort of grand ball-room. Rows of stained-glass windows adorned the arched white ceiling that was lined on either side by ornate chandeliers and tall, white columns. It was elegant and beautiful and pretty much the exact opposite of what Sam had expected to find in a casino.

"This is a casino?" Sam asked.

Charlotte smiled. But Sam could tell she was nervous about something.

"It used to be," she said. "In 1870, it was one of the most renowned gambling houses in the world. But that all shut down in the early 1900s. Fortunately, the building was preserved and it's now home to a host of charity events, weddings, and other things."

"Weddings?" Sam asked, thinking he could solve a murder and help his sister-in-law out at the same time.

"It's probably the most sought-after wedding venue in Saratoga," another voice said.

It was Gilford, who walked in behind Sam.

"You have to book it years in advance," he continued.

So much for saving the wedding, Sam thought.

"Sorry I'm late," Gilford said to Charlotte as he walked past Sam to stand next to her.

"I thought you were at the funeral home," Sam said.

"I left the same time you did," Gilford answered. "I can't have you talking to my client without me."

"What about you?" Sam asked Charlotte. "Why aren't you there?"

She shook her head. "I couldn't do it. I know it's silly, but it just makes it all seem so... final. I'll let the children sit through all of that stuff and then Arthur here can make the final arrangements later."

"So, what did you want to tell me?" Sam asked.

Charlotte looked at Gilford for reassurance. When he nodded, she continued.

"It's come to my attention that you and William discovered something suspicious in Frank's records."

Sam did a horrible job of hiding the shock on his face.

"He called Arthur as soon as you left," she explained. "And Arthur called me. I feel there's something you need to know, Mr. Lawson."

She motioned for Sam to join her at one of the small tables along the outer edge of the ballroom.

"Arthur also showed me the picture of the man you apprehended last night."

"Jimmy Goodwin," Sam said. "Do you recognize him?"

Charlotte stole another glance to Gilford, who nodded again.

"Yes," she said. "Jimmy is Frank's son."

Sam was sure his jaw hit the floor.

"He's what now?"

"The result of a regrettable indiscretion made early in our marriage. Before any of my children were born. It was a meaningless dalliance, but it bore fruit. I never even knew the mother's name. According to Frank, she was just visiting Saratoga for the weekend."

"She returned to tell Frank was pregnant," Gilford interjected. "He paid her off with a very large sum of money as long as she stayed away and kept his name out of it. I drew up the papers and she agreed.

"But when Jimmy grew up, he must have found out the truth," Sam said. "And that he had a rich dad."

"Frank was as suspicious, as are you," Charlotte said. "He had Arthur do some digging.

"Turns out his suspicions were right," Gilford chimed in. "Lots of petty crimes. A couple of felonies. He spent a little time in prison for identity theft."

"Yes, I'm well aware of his record," Sam said.

"Frank said he feared for me. Feared for the family.

He told Jimmy to leave, and he forbade me to contact him."

"But I'm guessing Jimmy didn't go away that easily," Sam said.

"Not at first," Gilford said. "But Frank knew Jimmy would have a price."

A light bulb turned on in Sam's head.

"So, Jimmy is Gold Paddock Consulting," he said.

Gilford nodded. "I would assume so."

"And I'm guessing it worked for a while," Sam said. "But what happened? Why did he come back."

"I'm assuming he wanted more money," Gilford added. "Frank told me that Mr. Goodwin texted him, saying he needed to meet. That happened the same day we met you at the track. I'm assuming Frank went to meet him later that night and that meeting is what was going on in the security footage you found."

"Why didn't you tell me any of this?" Sam asked.

"It was not mine to tell," Gilford said, walking behind Charlotte and putting a comforting hand on her shoulder.

"You've known this all along and you haven't said anything to me?" Sam asked, trying unsuccessfully to hide his anger. "When there was literally a loose Cannon out there?"

"You said yourself, that it must have been someone

in the house," Gilford replied. "We didn't think it would matter."

"First off, come on. Loose Cannon? Nothing?" Sam asked, wanting some acknowledgement for his bad pun. "Secondly, that's not when you 'begin to wonder'. That's when you stand up and say, 'I need to tell you something very important!'."

"Well, you know now," Gilford said.

Sam stood. "I just hope it's not too late."

64

SAM RUSHED BACK to the hotel to get his car. He needed to talk to Jimmy. He prayed he hadn't already been scared out of town and didn't want to risk doing it now. A phone call wouldn't do. Jimmy would almost certainly hang up on him. Plus, talking to him in person would give him the added advantage of reading his body language to ascertain what was the truth or a lie.

He thought about calling Durant, but decided to wait until he had a little bit more to go on before bringing in the police. Besides, if police came storming into Jimmy's hotel room, there's no telling what would happen. He needed to keep things cool, calm, and casual, or Jimmy would definitely clam up. Assuming he was still around.

Sam dodged traffic as he crossed Broadway and

looked for the hotel valet. Instead, he saw Natalie Edgars waiting on the steps of the hotel entrance. As soon as she saw him, she started walking toward him.

Sam let out an audible groan.

"I don't have time right now," he said.

He spotted the valet and gave him his ticket.

"I did some asking around," she said, ignoring him. "About the leak. And you were right. Six different local reporters all got an anonymous call within minutes of each other."

"Don't tell me," Sam said. "It was Arthur Gilford."

"No," Natalie replied. "It was a woman."

That got Sam's attention.

"It wasn't Gilford?" he asked. "Who was it?"

Natalie shook her head.

"No one was sure." she said. "But then I spoke to Dan Parker. Works for the local paper. He told me that he could have sworn it was Charlotte Cannon."

Sam was stunned.

"Charlotte?" he asked. "Frank's wife?"

"Frank's widow," Natalie corrected him. "But yeah. Dan spoke to her all the time about charity events and such, so he recognized her voice immediately. He even asked if it was her, but when he did, she hung up."

"Why didn't he report that?" Sam asked, still skeptical.

Natalie shrugged.

"He's been a Saratoga fixture forever," she said. "So has she. He probably didn't want to drag her name into it."

"But was happy to sell some papers based on a rumor."

"So, what do we do with this information?" Natalie asked.

Sam mulled it over as the valet arrived with his car.

"Sit on it for now," Sam said, walking around to the driver's door. "I'm on my way to check on a different lead that could help make sense of it all. And it will give you a bigger story."

"Let me come with you," she urged.

"No dice, kid," Sam said. "But I'll keep you updated. And nice work on the Charlotte lead."

Before Natalie could argue, he had shut the car door and driven away.

65

WHILE SAM KNEW the name of the motel where Jimmy was staying, he didn't know the room number and hoped the motel manager would be willing to help him. He walked up to the front desk and quickly flashed his PI badge, asking for Jimmy Goodwin's room with confidence.

The young woman behind the desk, with purple hair and piercings all over her face, was unimpressed. In fact, she barely looked up from her phone.

"You got a warrant?" she asked calmly without looking up.

"Warrant? I don't need a warrant," Sam said. "I'm not searching the place. I'm trying to find him."

The woman sighed, still not looking up.

"Our customers are entitled to their privacy," she said.

"So, he's still staying here?" Sam asked.

She looked up and glared at Sam as if daring him to say anything else. Sam pulled out his wallet and slid a twenty across the desk.

"All I want is the room number," he said. "I'll knock on his door and if he wants his privacy, he doesn't have to open it."

She took the money and returned to her phone.

"2F," she said.

Sam walked up the flight of stairs that ran along the outer edge of the motel. There were only six doors on the second floor, a white plastic chair sat outside of each one, accompanied by an old-fashioned brass ashtray stand, most of which looked as if they hadn't been emptied in weeks.

Sam heard a woman badly faking moans of pleasure from one of the rooms. He had a feeling that bad acting was costing someone by the hour.

The door to 2F was slightly ajar and it looked dark inside.

"Jimmy?" Sam yelled as he knocked. "You in there?"

The force of his knock pushed the door open further and Sam looked inside. The room was a disaster. Not from someone having ransacked it, but from someone never cleaning it up. The full-size bed was unmade, clothes were strewn all over the dark green carpet and the dresser top was littered with food wrappers and beer cans.

But there was no sign of Jimmy.

"Housekeeping," Sam yelled out, hoping that would get Jimmy's attention.

When no one responded, Sam stepped inside carefully. He instinctively reached for the gun in his shoulder holster, then remembered he was unarmed. He tried not to disturb the trash and dirty laundry as he carefully walked through the motel room toward the closed bathroom door.

He knocked on the door.

"Jimmy? You in there?"

Once again. No response.

He turned the doorknob and pushed the bathroom door open, flicking on the light immediately. While it was disgustingly filthy, there was no sign of Jimmy. Sam relaxed, letting out a sigh.

I'm too late, Sam thought. *He already left town.*

He walked back into the main room and looked around in hopes of miraculously finding any incriminating evidence. He knew none of it would be admissible in court, since technically he had entered the motel room unauthorized. But he could call Durant, who could investigate and confiscate any evidence legally.

Being careful not to touch anything, Sam scoured the dresser and bed for anything, without having any idea what he was looking for. Then he shifted his attention to the dirty clothes on the floor. Maybe some of them had Frank's blood on them.

He pushed the clothes around with his shoe, looking for any glimpse of red. That's when he noticed something under the bed.

Someone was hiding under the bed.

"Jimmy? Really?" Sam said as he dropped to his knees.

Sure enough. It was Jimmy. He was staring directly at Sam with a blank expression. Sam knew that look all too well.

Jimmy was dead.

66

S AM LEANED against one of the many police cars in the motel's parking lot, having finished giving his statement to one of the officers. A few motel guests had emerged and were sitting in their white plastic chairs, watching the proceedings. From their nonchalant behavior, Sam had the feeling they were used to this sort of thing.

He looked up at the crowd of law enforcement in what had been Jimmy's room. He had thought he had finally gotten a break in this case, but now his top suspect was dead. And murdered, no less. Shot point blank in the forehead. Now Sam was scrambling to figure out if this put him back at square one or actually got him closer to the truth. He decided he wanted to go back to the room and see what they were finding.

Another uniformed cop standing outside the door held out his hand to stop Sam until Detective Durant okayed his entry.

"So, what do you have?" Sam asked.

"Not much more than what you found," Durant replied. "Single shot to the forehead."

He moved toward the foot of the bed and pointed to a blood spatter on the curtains.

"Looks like the victim was standing here and facing his assailant."

"So, the assailant was further back in the room?" Sam asked.

Durant nodded.

"He could have already been hiding in the bathroom and surprised the victim, or he could have been talking to the victim and walked past him. It would help a lot if we knew how long the victim had been in his room."

"Do you have a time of death yet?" Sam asked.

"It's pretty fresh," Durant said. "Just a few hours. Tops."

"And there's no witnesses of anyone coming or going?" Sam asked.

Durant chuckled. "This is very much a 'mind-your-own-business' kind of motel, you know what I mean? And most guests weren't even around."

"What about security cameras on the street?" Sam asked. "You have any of those?"

Durant nodded. "We're trying to get access to those. It'll be a few hours, though. Hopefully, there's something there. But you can't see into the parking lot from the road and there is a path that takes you around back to a residential area. Someone could easily slip in and out of here. Hopefully, forensics will come up with something. But right now, we've got nothing."

Sam saw a cell phone in a transparent evidence bag on the counter.

"That his phone?"

"Yeah, it's password protected so we'll have to get tech to hack into it."

"There's answers in there," Sam said. "I'd count on it."

"How so?" Durant asked.

"For one, I doubt he just ran into Frank the other night," Sam answered. "That was a planned meeting. And they probably set it up via text."

"What about Frank's phone?"

"Y'all have it," Sam said. "You tell me. My guess is you looked and didn't see anything because he probably deleted it."

"Well, if he did, we can still access them. We'll need to get a warrant, but this incident and the security footage may give us enough probable cause for that."

Sam studied the phone again.

"This phone is the key," he mumbled to himself.

And then a smile spread across his face. He looked up at Durant.

"I think I have an idea. But you're going to have to trust me."

67

JULIA WAS the last to arrive to the Cannon house.

"What's this all about?" she asked Gilford as he led her into the living room where the rest of her family was already waiting.

Rebecca was sitting on one end of the couch while her mother sat on the other end. The space between them was noticeably empty. Peter had flopped down in the overstuffed brown leather chair and Donny sat in a smaller chair near the fireplace.

"Apparently, there's been a break in the case," William answered, scooting over on the loveseat to make room for his wife.

"Do we know what?" Julia asked.

"And couldn't he just have sent a group text?" Peter asked.

"Where's the fun in that?" Sam replied, emerging from the kitchen. "Besides, I needed you all in the same room."

"Why?" Charlotte asked.

"I'll get to that," Sam replied. He motioned for Gilford to take a seat as well, and the lawyer sat on the arm of the couch next to Charlotte.

"I suppose you all heard there was a murder in town today," Sam said, walking in front of the fireplace so that everyone was facing him.

"People are always getting killed at those motels," Peter said. "It's all meth heads and child molesters. Good riddance."

"Mr. Gilford, did you get a chance to show everyone the picture of Jimmy?" Sam asked.

Gilford hesitated.

"I didn't think so," Sam said. "It's okay. It's been a busy day."

Sam pulled a folded piece of paper from his pocket. It was the picture of Jimmy that Sam had shared with Gilford and Charlotte.

"Any of you recognize this man?" Sam asked, showing the picture to the group.

He handed it to Donny, who examined it before passing it around.

"His name's Jimmy Goodwin," Sam said.

Charlotte gasped, worried about what Sam was about to say.

"Should we care?" Peter asked.

"Why don't you ask your mother?" Sam replied.

Charlotte froze as all eyes turned to her. She looked up at Sam, her eyes pleading with him to not make her do this. Tears began to stream down her face as she opened her mouth to speak. But no words came out.

"Jimmy was your half-brother," Sam said, coaxing her along.

The room gasped. Everyone started asking questions all at once until Charlotte raised her hand to quiet them all down.

"It was before any of you were born," she said. "Your father made a mistake, but I forgave him. It was in our past and long forgotten and then... he just showed up one day."

"You never told us," Rebecca said.

"It was ancient history," Charlotte answered. "You all were his family."

"He was still our brother," William said. "We had a right to know."

"I know," Charlotte replied. "But your father forbade it. Over time, the memory just got lost in the life that followed. With all of you. Then, about a year ago, he showed up out of the blue."

"He smelled money," Peter said.

"That's what your father believed," Charlotte continued. "He wouldn't let me talk to him. Wouldn't let me say anything about it to any of you. I wanted to. You have to believe me."

"Mr. Lawson," Gilford interrupted. "You said 'WAS your half-brother'."

They all turned to Sam so suddenly, he took a step back.

"Goodwin was the person murdered today," Sam said quietly. "For the record, he wasn't a meth head or a child molester."

"You brought us here to tell us that?" Julia asked.

"Jesus, what kind of asshole are you?" William snapped.

"No," Sam replied. "I brought you here because one of you killed him."

68

ONCE AGAIN, the room erupted with questions and accusations. Sam yelled for them all to be quiet.

"Mr. Lawson," Gilford said. "May I remind you that you were hired to investigate Mr. Cannon's death, not this other man."

"This is true," Sam replied. "But I believe that Mr. Cannon and Jimmy were killed by the same person."

"What are you talking about?" William snapped. "We didn't even know about this Jimmy until just now."

"Some of you did," Sam replied. "You may not have known you were related, but you had dealings with him. What was the name of the company we were looking for? The location company or something?"

"Gold Paddock Consulting," Donny said.

Sam smiled and tapped his head.

"You and your photographic memory," he said. "That's right. Gold Paddock Consulting. I don't think it was real."

"You think it was Jimmy?" William asked.

"Why?" Donny asked.

"You think Dad was paying him off to keep him away?" William asked.

"And then he wanted more money, but Dad refused," Peter chimed in. "So, he killed him."

"That's what I thought at first, too," Sam said. "Until I saw his motel room. The man was not living large. My guess is, when we take a look at his bank records, there won't be any large monthly deposits."

"Plus, why would he kill Dad" William asked. "That cuts off his money supply completely."

"He could have just been pissed at him," Donny offered. "Wasn't thinking clearly."

"Possibly," Sam said. "But then who killed Jimmy?"

"Some random drug deal gone bad," Peter said. "That's not our problem."

"Other than the fact that he's your half-brother and you should probably care a little bit, I don't think that's the case," Sam said. "I don't think Jimmy killed your dad, but I think I know who did."

69

"LET'S start with the Gold Paddock payments," Sam said. "I don't think it was payoff money for Jimmy. I do, however, believe he knew about it.

"I did some digging and Jimmy was a bit of a computer whiz. Or should I say a bit of a computer hacker. Even did a little time for it. I believe he hacked into the Cannon bookkeeping system."

"That's impossible," Donny said.

"Not for someone that knew what they were doing," Sam said. "I believe he discovered the Gold Paddock payments and thought they looked suspicious."

"Why would he think that?" William asked.

"It's a working theory," Sam said. "Just go with me for now. What if Jimmy figured it out and, in order to win Frank over, decided to warn him about it. That's what they were meeting about in the alley the night your dad was murdered. And your dad refused to believe that someone would be stealing from him, so they argued."

"So, then who killed Dad?" Rebecca asked.

"Whoever didn't want anyone to know the truth about those payments."

"Dude, you're just making shit up now," Peter said.

Sam laughed.

"Yeah, it sounds like I'm grasping at straws, doesn't it?" Sam said, pulling an old black cell phone out of his pocket. "But then I found this in Jimmy's motel room."

"What is it?" Donny asked.

"Jimmy's cell phone," Sam said. "And it is filled with texts and phone numbers that back up my theory. And identify the killer."

"Did you take that from the crime scene?" Gilford asked. "Shouldn't that be evidence?"

Sam shrugged.

"I borrowed it," he said. "You know, for a person as mysterious as Jimmy, you'd think he'd come up with a better passcode than 1234."

"So, what's on it?" Rebecca asked, scooting to the edge of the couch.

"There are texts from Frank," Sam said. "Jimmy had his name in the contacts, so he was easy to spot. And it turns out they did arrange to meet early Wednesday morning."

Sam opened the phone and read from it.

"This is a text to Frank. 'There's something you need to know. Meet me tonight behind Tessa's.'"

"Does it say what he needed to know?" William asked. "Is that in the texts?"

Sam shook his head. "Sadly, no. And that was their last communication."

"Then you don't know anything!" Peter exclaimed.

"Well, that's not the interesting texts," Sam said. "There's another text chain with someone else, they're not in the contacts so it's just a number. Lots of mysterious messages to this number. And they all start after Frank Cannon died. Pretty threatening, actually."

"Who does the number belong to?" Charlotte asked.

"Don't know yet," Sam said. "But that's why I wanted you all to meet me here. I'm assuming you all have your phones with you."

Everyone looked at each other.

"I figured I could just dial the number," Sam said. "And we'll see whose phone rings."

70

SAM SLOWLY DIALED a number into the phone, looking around at everyone as he did.

The whole family was looking around at each other, trying to figure out whose phone would ring. Everyone but Donny, who was staring at the phone in Sam's hand. Sam noticed the beads of sweat forming on Donny's forehead. He stopped dialing and smiled.

"Are you really going to make me go through with this, Donny?" he said.

"Donny?" Rebecca gasped.

"I don't know what he's talking about," Donny stammered.

"What the hell did you do?" William asked.

"Frank wasn't paying Jimmy off. He didn't even

know about Gold Paddock," Sam said, turning his attention to Donny.

"I remember something William said to me about how you have this photographic memory about payments. A walking computer, wasn't that what you said?"

William nodded, never taking his eyes off Donny.

"You said that all payments went through him to the point that Frank didn't even need a checkbook. What was the phrase? 'Dad didn't even get a snack from the vending machine without checking with Donny'."

"Well, he clearly made those payments from his account," Donny argued.

"The account that you managed?" Sam asked. "And you didn't notice a $10,000 payment each month?"

"I noticed," Donny said. "And Frank told me they were for a location consultant."

"Then why, when William and I asked you about the payments, did you not know what they were at first?" Sam asked.

"Yeah," William said. "I remember. You had to look it up. Now that I think about it, that was weird. You never have to look anything up."

"I wanted to make sure," Donny argued.

"I'm sorry," Charlotte said. "What are you insinuating here?"

"Donny was skimming," William said. "He was

stealing ten thousand bucks a month, right under our nose."

"Come on," Donny said. "You're not buying any of this, are you?"

"Jimmy figured it out," Sam said, holding the phone up again. "He didn't know who was doing it, but he knew someone was. He figured it was the kind of news that could score him points with Frank, so he arranged to tell him that night in the alley."

Sam pointed to the couch where Rebecca and Charlotte were sitting.

"You were on that couch that night. Right?"

Donny nodded.

"You heard Frank turn off the security system and sneak out, so you decided to follow him."

"Why would I do that?" Donny asked.

"Guilty conscience? A little paranoid?" Sam suggested. "When most people commit a crime, they begin to worry who knows. They assume the worst about everything. So, when you saw him sneaking out, you needed to know why."

"Well, that's a stretch," Donny said, turning to everyone in the room. "This is total fiction."

"When you overheard the conversation in the alley, it confirmed your fears. You knew you needed to act fast to cover your crime, so you rushed back to the house, hid behind the curtain in the office and then killed Frank before he could expose you."

"You're insane!" Donny yelled.

"Except Jimmy saw you in the alley," Sam continued. "And when he found out about Frank's death, he knew it wasn't a coincidence. He not only figured out you were Gold Paddock Consulting, but also that you were the killer."

"He was going to turn you in," Charlotte sneered. "He barely knew us, and he was more loyal than you."

"He wasn't loyal," Donny snapped. "He wanted a cut. He wanted half the money to keep his mouth shut."

Everyone gasped and Donny froze, realizing what he had just said.

71

Donny shook his head in resignation.

"I didn't mean for it to happen," he said quietly. "I was just going to delete the files. But then he got home before I could do it, so I hid behind the curtain. I figured he'd just go to bed but then he came into the office."

"I can't believe I'm hearing this," William said, staring in shock at his best friend.

"He sat down and started going through the records, writing down every Gold Paddocks payment," Donny said. "I panicked. I knew he was going to figure out it was me. And then it all got blurry."

Tears streamed down Donny's face and his voice trembled.

338 DAVID K WILSON

"The next thing I knew, I was grabbing that knife on his credenza and ...."

He dropped his head in his hands.

"I'm so sorry," he cried.

"You son of a bitch," William yelled.

He lunged toward his friend, but Sam jumped in the way.

"Stand down," Sam said, one hand on William's chest.

William pushed his anger down and slapped Sam's hand away before returning to his seat.

"So, what did you do next?" Sam asked.

"I don't know," Donny muttered. "Luckily, Frank was true to form and forgot to reset the alarm when he came home. So, I took his laptop and the notes he'd written, wiped the room for my prints, then snuck out of the house, went to my place, and changed clothes, then dropped the laptop off at the dealership. I got back around 4, re-set the alarm and pretended to go back to sleep."

"And when the police ruled it a suicide, you thought you had got away with it," Sam said, waving the phone. "But then Jimmy started texting you."

"Should have known he'd be as greedy as the rest of you," Donny snapped, his remorse turning into resentment. "You know what it's like watching all of you? Entitled. Spoiled. Assholes. I deserved my share."

William stood up again.

"You jackass. You were paid well!"

"I was paid competitively for my job title," Donny said. "Meanwhile, he's making you a VP and Jackie a VP. I couldn't even get a CFO title."

"Is that all you wanted?" William yelled. "A title?"

"I wanted get paid a CFO's salary!" Donny yelled back.

"You needed the money, didn't you?" Sam guessed. "Probably have some gambling debts that were pulling you under?"

"That's no one's business but mine," Donny said. "I worked my ass off and I still made less than what Peter got, who doesn't even know how to work. Or Julia, who blows it on horses and her side piece."

William turned to his wife stunned. She shook her head in denial but looked guilty as hell.

"Or my lovely ex-wife," Donny continued ranting. "Who just chews up and spits out people like they're nothing."

"So, Jimmy wanted half," Sam said, trying to steer the conversation back around. "But you didn't want to share, did you? Even more importantly, he was a loose end. You'd always have to worry about him going to the police."

"I had no choice," Donny said. "I was in too deep to let him mess it up."

"You killed my Frank," Charlotte stammered.

"I'm gonna kill you," William yelled, lunging for Donny again.

He grabbed him by the throat as Sam and Julia tried to wrestle him off. Donny finally writhed away and punched William in the face. William looked at him in shock. Donny, his face pinched in boiling anger cocked his arm to throw another punch. But before he could, Rebecca hit him over the head with a bottle of bourbon. Donny instantly collapsed to the floor.

"Oh, that's gonna leave a mark," Sam said as he pulled the half-conscious Donny to a chair.

"You stole that phone from a crime scene," Donny said. "Those texts won't be allowed in court."

Sam looked at the phone and grinned.

"Oh, this? This is just a cheap knock-off I picked up at the Salvation Army. Doesn't even work."

He showed the black screen to a stunned Donny then pulled his own phone from a chest pocket.

"This one, on the other hand, is very real. And it recorded everything."

72

DETECTIVE DURANT and three uniformed officers barged in the front door. Sam looked at Durant with a big grin.

"You get it all?" he asked.

"Crystal clear," Durant said, helping Donny to his feet and cuffing his hands behind his back.

Donny looked at Durant and then at Sam. In answer to the question Donny was no doubt thinking, Sam lifted his shirt to reveal the mic taped to his chest.

"You can't trust phones," he said.

"How did you know it was him?" Durant asked. "If you would have said anything wrong, he would have known you were bluffing."

Sam shrugged. "I played a hunch. I knew he had a

photographic memory but hoped that if I was close, he would start second-guessing the exact words."

"How long have you known?" Donny asked.

"I honestly wasn't sure until you admitted it," Sam said. "I actually had my money on Charlotte. But when I found out she was the one that leaked the possibility that Frank was murdered, I had to second guess. If she had done it, she would not have wanted to turn up the heat. Honestly, I'm just relieved it was someone in the room. Otherwise, this whole little charade would have been very awkward."

Durant began to read Donny his rights as he led him away. As two tech officers descended upon Sam to remove the wire and take his phone.

"I'm gonna need that back," he said as they bagged the equipment and walked away. "And don't check my search history."

He leaned back on the banquette seat of the large bay window and took a deep breath, realizing for the first time how hard his heart was pounding. Durant returned shortly and sat beside him. He nodded toward William and Julia who were huddled in a corner having a hushed argument.

"Can't imagine what those two are talking about," Sam said.

"Yeah, you really opened a a big can of worms today," Durant replied.

"For the record, Donny is the one that opened that particular can," Sam said with a laugh before turning sincere. "Hey. Thanks for trusting me."

Durant sighed. "I was wrong. You were right. The important thing is the truth came out and hopefully justice will be served. That's way more important than getting a little egg on my face."

"What about your chief?" Sam asked. "He's not gonna like this."

"Oh, he's definitely not going to like this," Durant replied with a chuckle. "And I'll most likely be the scapegoat."

"We'll deal with Chief Morelli, Detective," Gilford said as he and Charlotte approached.

"Sam told us how you haven't let this case go," Charlotte said. "Even when it wasn't in your best interest. Thank you."

Durant nodded. "I'm just sorry I made the wrong call at first. You all deserved better."

A uniformed officer called Durant away and he excused himself.

Charlotte and Gilford turned to Sam.

"Mr. Lawson, I can't thank you enough for all you've done," Charlotte said.

"Sorry about the mess," Sam replied.

He glanced over at William and Julia just as William stormed away.

"All you did was shine a light on some things that needed to be out in the open," she replied. "As painful as all of that is, it's for the best."

"I'll have your payment sent to the hotel immediately, along with a handsome bonus," Gilford said. "And please keep the car for the duration of your stay in Saratoga."

Sam shook his head.

"You can have the car back," he said. "Unless you're willing to pay my valet bill at the hotel. Otherwise, All I'll be doing is driving around and look for parking places."

"We'll take care of the valet bill," Gilford said. "And your hotel bill."

"And if there's anything we can do for you," Charlotte said. "Please don't hesitate to ask."

Sam nodded and shook both of their hands. But, as they turned to walk away, Sam stopped them.

"Actually, there are a couple of things."

73

SAM BARELY HEARD the ping on his newly returned phone as he watched the 14-piece band belt out another 80s classic to the delight of the dancing crowd. It was a text from Natalie with a link. Sam opened it to a news article on the WSXI website with a video showing Natalie reporting in front of the Cannon house. The headline under the video read:

AN INSIDE LOOK INTO THE CANNON MURDER INVESTIGATION

Exclusive interview with Charlotte Cannon

As he read, a follow-up text appeared.

CNN HAS REACHED OUT AND WANTS TO TALK TO ME ABOUT THE INTERVIEW!! THANK YOU FOR SETTING IT UP!!!

Sam smiled and put his phone away. As a server

walked by with a tray of hors d'oeuvres, he nabbed one without even looking at it.

"Ooh, what's this one?" he asked, examining the unfamiliar object.

"Broiled goat cheese toast with marinated greens," the waitress answered with a smile.

Sam gamefully plopped it in his mouth and immediately regretted it.

"Don't mind him," Carla said to the server as she walked up next to her husband. "We don't let him out in public that often."

The server smiled and walked away.

"Sam this is all so wonderful," she said. "Vanessa is beside herself."

Sam smiled but was only half listening. He was lost in admiration of his beautiful wife. She was stunning in her elegant satin maroon dress and hair pulled back loosely, a curled wisp falling gracefully across her cheek.

"You are so beautiful," Sam said.

They kissed just as Vanessa and Ray danced over. Vanessa, in a soft white off-shoulder gown, threw her arms around Sam. A tuxedoed Ray shook his hand.

"Thank you so much for all of this," Vanessa said. "I mean, our wedding reception at the Canfield Casino! And at the last minute!"

"It wasn't me," Sam said. "This is all Charlotte Cannon."

"Yeah, but as a thank you to you," Ray said.

"She took care of everything," Vanessa said. "The decorations. The catering. Even the band."

A server stopped in front of them with a tray of crackers and cheese.

"Oooh!" Vanessa said, lifting one from the tray. "Thank you."

"Is that more goat cheese?" Sam asked again.

"Sam," Carla interrupted.

"It's feta, sir," the server replied.

"But it's not regular cheese, right?" Sam asked.

"Not a feta fan?" Ray asked.

"I only like cheese from cows," Sam said with total seriousness. "Other animals just don't make it the same."

"Mr. Sophisticated," Carla teased.

"No. I'm with you, Sam," Ray said. "Have you had the steak frite bites?"

He looked around the banquet hall and waved a server to them.

"I guarantee you will like these," he said as the server approached.

Sam saw the tray approaching, his eyes widening.

"It's really steak?" he asked.

"Little strips of steak wrapped around fries," Ray said.

Sam sampled one, moaning in approval.

"Never leave my side," he said to the server.

"Oh my God," Carla laughed. "He has never looked at me that way."

Just as Sam reached for another, the band started playing a Van Morrison ballad. Carla grabbed his arm.

"Dance with me," she said.

Sam plopped the bite into his mouth and turned to the waiter. "Wait right here. And guard these with your life."

He and Carla walked to the dance floor, and she circled her arms around his neck. They swayed back and forth to the music, his arms around her waist, lost in each other's eyes. Sam finally broke the silence.

"Have I told you lately how much I love you?" Sam asked.

"You're just happy you got some food you like," Carla teased.

"I'll be happier when you actually let me eat it," Sam replied.

They continued to dance silently, basking in each other's arms.

"This is nice," Carla said. "Just peace and calm."

Sam chuckled. "We haven't had much of that recently, have we?"

Carla rested her head on Sam's shoulder and closed her eyes, savoring the moment. And then she grinned. She lifted her head and looked him in the eyes.

"That actually sounds boring as hell."

Sam breathed a sigh of relief.

"Thank God," he said. "I think I'd actually go crazy."

The two laughed and he spun her around before pulling her close again.

THANK YOU FOR READING
MURDER IN SPA CITY

If you enjoyed it, please leave a review on Amazon.com or Goodreads, or wherever you purchased your copy. A review can go a long way in helping other readers find this book.

GET A FREE COPY OF *BOUND BY MURDER*
This fun and riveting mystery novella e-book is available for free at **davidkwilsonauthor.com**

ENJOY THESE OTHER SAM LAWSON MYSTERIES:

ALSO BY DAVID K. WILSON:

RED DIRT BLUES

"Wildly entertaining and absurdly funny!"

A cold-blooded thief finds herself pulled into the quirky and colorful lives of a motley crew of rednecks.

ACKNOWLEDGMENTS

It takes a village to birth a book and I'm fortunate enough to have an amazing tribe of villagers, starting with my team of first readers: Shelley Upchurch, Lorraine Evanoff, Yvonne Pelletier, James Hewitson, Barbara Fournier, April Weygand and Jon Wurtmann. Also, a special shout out to Doug Jetter for some non-racing tips about the Saratoga Race Track.

Of course, nothing happens without the consent of the Dynamic Duo, Regina Riddle and Rena Grubbs. My gratitude for their constant support and friendship - and always keeping me East Texas honest - extends way beyond words.

Speaking of gratitude, I am eternally thankful for the creative artistry of my cover designer Carolyn Johnson. Once again, she has elevated my book to an unimaginable level.

I can't forget my biggest cheerleader, unofficial publicist and incredible friend, Jo-Ann Lant. Thanks for all your support.

Finally, thanks to all my other friends and family

who continue to support me, including my incredible parents, Jim and Barbara Wilson, and three amazing kids, Alayna, Colin and Mallory. I know you're all way too old to still be called kids, but you're definitely not children and 'offspring' just sounds weird.

ABOUT THE AUTHOR

David K. Wilson grew up in East Texas, surrounded by enough colorful characters to fill the pages of hundreds of books. In addition to being the author of the popular Sam Lawson Mystery series and the highly lauded crime comedy, *Red Dirt Blues*, David is also a seasoned ghostwriter and screenwriter. He currently lives in upstate New York.

Sign up to receive updates on David's next novel at davidkwilsonauthor.com.

facebook.com/davidkwilsonauthor

instagram.com/davidkwilsonauthor

goodreads.com/davidkwilson

Made in the USA
Coppell, TX
11 August 2024

35875027R00215